A Treasury of Disney
Little Golden Books®
22 Best-Loved Disney Stories

A GOLDEN BOOK • NEW YORK

Western Publishing Company, Inc., Racine, Wisconsin 53404

Contents

Snow White and the Seven Dwarfs

Long ago, in a faraway kingdom, there lived a lovely young princess named Snow White.

Her stepmother, the queen, was cruel and vain. She hated anyone whose beauty rivaled her own—and she watched her stepdaughter with angry, jealous eyes.

The queen had magic powers and owned a wondrous mirror that spoke. Every day she stood before it and asked:

> "Magic mirror on the wall,
>   Who is the fairest one of all?"

And every day the mirror answered:

> "You are the fairest of all, O Queen,
>   The fairest our eyes have ever seen."

As time passed, Snow White grew more and more beautiful—and the queen grew more and more envious. So she forced the princess to dress in rags and work in the kitchen from dawn to dusk.

Despite all the hard work, Snow White stayed sweet, gentle, and cheerful.

Day after day she dreamed of a handsome prince who would come and carry her off to his castle.

One day when the queen spoke to her mirror, it replied with the words she had been dreading:

> "Fair is thy beauty, Majesty,
>   But hold—a lovely maid I see,
>   One who is more fair than thee.
>   Lips red as a rose, hair black as ebony,
>   skin white as snow..."

The unhappy man begged the queen to be merciful, but she would not be persuaded. "Remember my magic powers," she warned. "Obey me, or you and your family will suffer!"

The next day Snow White, never suspecting that she was in danger, went off with the huntsman.

When they were deep in the woods, the huntsman drew his knife. Then, suddenly, he fell to his knees.

"I can't kill you," he sobbed. "Forgive me, sweet Princess. It was the queen who ordered this wicked deed."

"The queen?" gasped Snow White.

"She's mad with jealousy," said the huntsman. "She'll stop at nothing to destroy you. Quick—run away and don't come back. I'll lie to the queen. Now go! Run! Save yourself!"

Frightened, Snow White fled through the woods.

Tangled branches tore at her clothes. Sharp twigs scratched her arms and legs. Strange eyes stared from the shadows. Danger lurked everywhere.

Snow White ran on and on.

At last Snow White fell wearily to the ground and began to weep. The gentle animals of the forest gathered around and tried to comfort her.

"Snow White?" shrieked the angry queen. "She must be destroyed!"

The queen sent for her huntsman.

"Take Snow White deep into the forest," she said, "and there, my faithful one, kill her."

The animals all helped, and soon the place was spick-and-span.

Meanwhile, the Seven Dwarfs who lived in the cottage were starting home from the mine where they worked. On their way they sang:

"Heigh-ho, heigh-ho,
It's home from work we go..."

The dwarfs were amazed to find their house so neat and clean. They were even more amazed when they tiptoed upstairs and saw Snow White!

"A gleeping sirl—I mean, a sleeping girl!" said the dwarf called Doc.

"She's purty," said the one named Sneezy.

Chirping and chattering, they led her to a tiny cottage.

"Oh," said Snow White, "how sweet! It's just like a doll's house."

But inside, the little tables and chairs were covered with dust, and the sink was filled with dirty dishes.

"My!" said Snow White. "Perhaps the children who live here are orphans and need someone to take care of them. Let's tidy everything up. Maybe they'll let me stay and keep house for them."

"B-beautiful," sighed Bashful.

"Bah!" said Grumpy. "She's going to be trouble! Mark my words!"

Snow White woke up with a start. "Why, you're not children," she said when she saw the dwarfs. "You're little men!"

The dwarfs gathered around her.

"I read your names on the beds," said Snow White. "Let me guess who you are. You must be Doc. And you must be Bashful. Then there's Sneezy, and Sleepy, and Happy, and Dopey...and *you* must be Grumpy!"

When Snow White told the dwarfs of the queen's plan to kill her, they decided that she should stay with them.

"We're askin' for trouble," huffed Grumpy.

9

"But we *can't* let her be caught by that kwicked ween—I mean, wicked queen!" said Doc. The others all agreed.

That night, after supper, they all sang and danced and made merry music. Bashful played the concertina. Happy tapped the drums. Sleepy tooted the horn. Grumpy played the organ. Dopey didn't know how to sing or play a tune, but he was very good at wiggling his ears!

Snow White loved her new friends. And she felt safe at last.

But the queen had learned from her mirror that Snow White was still alive. "This time," she hissed, "I'll finish her!"

With a magic spell, she turned herself into an old peddler woman. She filled a basket with apples, putting a poisoned apple on top.

"One bite," she cackled, "and Snow White will sleep forever. Then *I* will be the fairest in the land!"

Next morning, before they left for the mine, the dwarfs warned Snow White to be on her guard.

"Beware of strangers," said Doc.

"Right," said Grumpy. "Don't let nobody or nothin' in the house."

"Oh, Grumpy," said Snow White, "you *do* care! I'll be careful, I promise." She kissed him and the others good-bye, and the dwarfs went cheerfully off to work.

A few minutes later the queen came to the kitchen window.

"Baking pies, dearie?" she asked. "It's *apple* pies the men love. Here, taste one of these." She held the poisoned apple out to Snow White.

Snow White remembered the dwarfs' warning. "But what harm can a poor old woman do?" she thought. "And that apple does look delicious."

She bit the poisoned apple. Then, with a sigh, she fell to the floor.

After being told by the birds and animals that something was wrong, the dwarfs raced back to the cottage. They saw the queen sneaking off, and they ran after her.

As storm clouds gathered and rain began to fall, the dwarfs chased the queen up a high, rocky mountain. Up, up they went, to the very top.

Crack! There was a flash of lightning, and the evil queen fell to her doom below.

But it was too late for Snow White. She was so beautiful, even in death, that the dwarfs could not bear to part with her. They built her a coffin of glass and gold, and day and night they kept watch over their beloved princess.

One day a handsome prince came riding through the forest. As soon as he saw Snow White he fell in love with her. Kneeling by her coffin, he kissed her.

Snow White sat up, blinked her eyes, and smiled. The prince's kiss had broken the evil spell!

As the dwarfs danced with joy the prince carried Snow White off to his castle, where they lived happily ever after.

Cinderella ✓

Once upon a time, in a faraway kingdom, there lived a widowed gentleman and his lovely daughter, Ella.

Ella was a beautiful girl. She had golden hair, and her eyes were as blue as forget-me-nots.

The gentleman was a kind and devoted father, and he gave Ella everything her heart desired. But he felt she needed a mother. So he married again, choosing for his wife a woman who had two daughters. Their names were Anastasia and Drizella.

The gentleman soon died. Then the stepmother's true nature was revealed. She was only interested in her ugly, selfish daughters.

The stepmother gave Ella a little room in the attic, old rags to wear, and all the housework to do. Soon everyone called her Cinderella, because she got so covered with cinders from cleaning the fireplaces.

But Cinderella had many friends. The old horse and Bruno the dog loved her. The mice loved her, too. She protected them from her stepmother's nasty cat, Lucifer. Two of her favorite mice were Gus and Jaq.

Cinderella was kind to everyone—even to Lucifer. But Lucifer only took advantage of her kindness.

Lucifer liked to get Cinderella in trouble. One morning he chased Gus onto Anastasia's breakfast tray. She screamed and blamed Cinderella.

"As punishment," the stepmother said to Cinderella, "you will wash the windows, scrub the terrace, and sweep the halls. And don't forget the laundry."

In another part of the kingdom the king was worrying about his son. "It's time the prince got married!" he told the grand duke.

"But, sire," said the grand duke, "he must fall in love first."

"No buts about it! We'll have a ball tonight. It will be very romantic. Send out the invitations!"

When the invitation arrived, Cinderella's stepmother announced, "Every girl in the kingdom is invited to a ball in honor of the prince."

"Why, that means I can go, too," Cinderella said.

"Well, yes," the stepmother replied with a sly smile. "But *only* if you get all your work done, and *only* if you have something suitable to wear."

Cinderella had hoped to fix her old party dress, but Anastasia and Drizella wanted her to help them, instead. The stepmother kept her busy, too.

Cinderella worked hard all day long. When she finally came back to her little attic room, it was almost time to leave for the ball. And she realized her dress wasn't ready!

But the mice had managed to find ribbons, sashes, ruffles, and bows. The mice had sewn them to her party dress, and it looked beautiful.

The stepsisters shrieked when they saw Cinderella.

"Those are my ribbons!" "That is my sash!" They tore her dress to shreds.

"Come along now, girls," said the stepmother.

Cinderella ran into the garden. She wept and wept.

Suddenly a hush fell over the garden, and a cloud of lights began to twinkle and glow around Cinderella's head.

"Come on, dry those tears," said a gentle voice. Then a small woman appeared in the cloud. "You can't go to the ball like that. Now, where's my magic wand?"

"Magic wand?" gasped Cinderella. "Are you my..."

"Fairy godmother," the woman replied, pulling her magic wand out of thin air. "What we need is a pumpkin."

A cloud of sparkles floated across the garden. A pumpkin rose up and swelled into an elegant coach. The mice turned into horses, the old horse became a coachman, and Bruno became a footman.

"Now, off you go, dearie," said the woman.

"But my dress..." said Cinderella.

The fairy godmother looked at it. "Good heavens!" With a wave of her wand, she turned Cinderella's rags into an exquisite gown. On Cinderella's feet were tiny glass slippers.

"Now, remember," the fairy godmother said, "you must leave the ball at midnight. That's when the spell will be broken and all will be as it was before."

Cinderella promised. Then she stepped into her magical coach and was swept away to the palace.

When Cinderella arrived at the ball, the prince was yawning with boredom. Then he caught sight of her.

Ignoring everything around him, the prince walked over to her. He kissed Cinderella's hand and asked her to dance. They swirled off across the ballroom.

The prince never left Cinderella's side. They danced every dance together. As everyone watched them the lights dimmed and sweet music floated out into the summer night.

And then Cinderella heard the clock begin to chime.

"Oh, no!" she gasped. "It's midnight. I must go!"

"Wait! Come back!" called the prince.

Cinderella hurried down the palace steps. In her haste, she lost one of the glass slippers, but she had no time to pick it up. She leapt into the waiting coach.

As soon as the coach went through the gates, the magic spell broke. Cinderella found herself standing by the side of the road, dressed in her old rags. On her foot, she still wore the other glass slipper.

Her coachman was an old horse again, and her footman was Bruno the dog. Her coach was an old hollow pumpkin, and her horses were four of her mouse friends. They looked sadly at Cinderella.

Then they all hurried home before the others returned from the ball.

The next day, the stepmother told the girls that the grand duke was coming to see them. "He's searching the kingdom for the young lady whose foot fits the slipper. Whoever she is, she will marry the prince."

Cinderella smiled and hummed the very waltz that had been played at the ball. The stepmother became suspicious. She locked Cinderella in her room.

Gus and Jaq had a plan to help Cinderella. While Anastasia and Drizella tried to squeeze their big feet into the little glass slipper, the two mice sneaked into the stepmother's pocket. They got hold of the key, tugged it up the stairs, and unlocked the door. Cinderella rushed downstairs to try on the glass slipper.

"Your Grace," she said, "may I try on the slipper?"

The wicked stepmother fumed with anger. She tripped the page who was holding the glass slipper. It fell to the floor and broke into a thousand pieces.

"Don't worry," Cinderella said, reaching into her pocket. "I have the other one right here."

She put on the slipper, and it fitted perfectly.

From that moment on, everything was a dream come true. Cinderella went off to the palace with the happy grand duke. The prince was overjoyed to see her, and so was the king. Cinderella and the prince were soon married.

In her happiness, Cinderella didn't forget about her animal friends. They all moved into the castle.

Everyone in the kingdom was delighted with the prince's new bride. And Cinderella and the prince lived happily ever after!

Alice in Wonderland Meets the White Rabbit

Do you know where Wonderland is? It is the place you visit in your dreams, the strange and wondrous place where nothing is as it seems. It was in Wonderland that Alice met the White Rabbit.

He was hurrying across the meadow, looking at his pocket watch and saying to himself, "I'm late, I'm late, for an important date."

So Alice followed him.

"What a peculiar place to give a party," she thought as she pushed her way into the hollow tree.

But before she could think any more, she began to slide on some slippery white pebbles inside. And then she began to fall!

"Curious and curiouser!" said Alice as she floated slowly down, past cupboards and lamps, a rocking chair, past clocks and mirrors she met in midair.

By the time she reached the bottom, and landed with a thump, the White Rabbit was disappearing through a tiny door, too small for Alice to follow him.

Poor Alice! She was all alone in Wonderland, where nothing was just what it seemed. (You know how things are in dreams!)

At last she reached a neat little house in the woods, with pink shutters and a little front door that opened and—out came the White Rabbit!

She met other animals, yes, indeed, strange talking animals, too. They tried to be as helpful as they could. But they couldn't help her find the White Rabbit.

"And I really must find him," Alice thought, though she wasn't sure just why.

So on she wandered through Wonderland, all by her lonely self.

"Oh, my twitching whiskers!" he was saying to himself. He seemed very much upset. Then he looked up and saw Alice standing there.

"Mary Ann!" he said sharply. "Why, Mary Ann, what are you doing here? Well, don't just do something, stand there! No, go get my gloves. I'm very late!"

"But late for what? That's just what I—" Alice began to ask.

"My gloves!" said the White Rabbit firmly.

And Alice dutifully went to look for them, though she knew she wasn't Mary Ann!

When she came back, the White Rabbit was just disappearing through the woods again.

So off went Alice, trying to follow him through that strange, mixed-up Wonderland.

She met Tweedledee and Tweedledum, a funny little pair.

She joined a mad tea party with the Mad Hatter and the March Hare.

She met a Cheshire cat who faded in and out of sight. And one strange creature—Jabberwock—whose eyes flamed in the night.

They all were very kind, but they could not show Alice the way, until—

"There *is* a shortcut," she heard the Cheshire cat say. So Alice took it.

The shortcut led into a garden where gardeners were busy painting roses red.

"We must hurry," they said, "for the queen is coming!"

And sure enough a trumpet blew, and a voice called:

"Make way for the Queen of Hearts!"

Then out came a grand procession. And who should be the royal trumpeter for the cross-looking queen but the White Rabbit, all dressed up and looking very fine.

"Well!" said Alice. "So this is why he was hurrying so!"

"Who are you?" snapped the queen. "Do you play croquet?"

"I'm Alice. And I'm just on my way home. Thank you for the invitation, but I really mustn't stay."

"So!" cried the queen. "So she won't play! Off with her head, then!"

But Alice was tired of Wonderland now and all its nonsensical ways.

"Pooh!" she said. "I'm not frightened of you. You're nothing but a pack of cards."

And with that she ran back through that land of dreams, back to the riverbank where she had fallen asleep.

"Hmm," she said as she rubbed her eyes. "I'm glad to be back where things are what they seem. I've had quite enough for now of Wonderland!"

Peter Pan ✓

There was a place, a faraway place, where the sun always shone, the sky was always blue, and no one ever grew old. This place was called Never Land, and it was where Peter Pan and Tinker Bell lived.

Not so very far away, in the city of London, lived John, Wendy, and Michael Darling. Every night they would gather in the nursery to hear Wendy tell wonderful tales of Peter Pan's adventures with friendly Indians and nasty pirates in Never Land.

One night, when Wendy was telling John and Michael a favorite Peter Pan story, Nana, their Saint Bernard, started barking outside in the yard. Not a moment later Peter Pan appeared with Tinker Bell.

"I came to find my shadow," said Peter Pan. "Nana took it from me the other night as I was secretly listening to your stories."

"Here it is," said Wendy. John and Michael looked on in amazement as she sewed it back on to Peter's body.

"I'm so glad we saw you tonight, Peter," Wendy said. "You see, tonight's my last night in the nursery, because tomorrow I have to grow up."

"But that means no more stories," cried Peter, "unless I take you all back to Never Land with me!"

Wendy, John, and Michael couldn't believe their ears. "That would be wonderful!" they shouted.

Peter Pan sprinkled some of Tinker Bell's pixie dust over the children and told them to think happy thoughts.

"Now you can fly!" said Peter.

Suddenly they were all soaring through the skies of London, heading directly toward Never Land.

Down below they saw golden rainbows and blue waterfalls and mermaids singing in a lagoon. It was the most beautiful place they had ever seen. There were beaches and deep forests and, of course, there was the Indian camp! Yes, this indeed was Never Land.

"This way," called Peter Pan as Wendy, John, and Michael landed in one of the forests. He led them to the secret underground home where he lived with his good friends the Lost Boys.

John and Michael played with the boys while Peter and Wendy went to visit the beautiful mermaids in the lagoon.

were coming up from underground. One by one they were captured and taken to the pirate ship.

"Peter Pan will save us," Wendy said bravely.

Captain Hook roared with wicked laughter. "Pan will never be able to save you," he shouted. "You will walk the plank!"

No one noticed as Tinker Bell escaped from the lantern. She flew as fast as she could to alert Peter Pan.

It was there that Peter Pan spied the Indian chief's daughter, Tiger Lily, tied up in the boat of the evil Captain Hook.

Peter and Wendy could overhear the pirate demanding, "Tell me the hiding place of Peter Pan!" But Tiger Lily wouldn't tell.

"I have to save her," Peter told Wendy. They flew off together to Skull Rock, where Captain Hook had taken Tiger Lily.

There, Peter challenged Captain Hook to a thrilling duel. Peter was so quick and brave that at last the nasty pirate landed in the water, only to be chased back to his ship by a ferocious crocodile. Peter rescued Tiger Lily and returned her to her father, the chief.

Captain Hook was very angry. "That cursed Peter Pan! I shall have my revenge against him once and for all!" he cried.

He captured Tinker Bell and forced her to show him where Peter Pan lived. Then he caged her in a lantern!

As Captain Hook's band of pirates approached Peter Pan's home, the Darlings and the Lost Boys

Once Tinker Bell reached Peter Pan, he raced out to sea to rescue his friends. "I've come to stop you once and for all, Captain Hook!" cried Peter. "This time you've gone too far!"

After another fierce duel, Peter Pan threw Hook and all the pirates overboard. Hook was chased away by the crocodile, and nobody cared to save him!

"Thank you ever so much for rescuing us, Peter," said Wendy. "We would love to stay in Never Land awhile longer, but it's getting late and I think it's time for us to leave." John and Michael nodded in agreement.

"Well, if that's the case," said Peter, "we sail tonight!"

Once again Peter Pan sprinkled Tinker Bell's pixie dust over everyone, and Captain Hook's pirate ship was suddenly sailing through the skies of Never Land, heading back to the Darlings' home in London.

But before Peter Pan and Tinker Bell started off for Never Land, they made Wendy, John, and Michael promise never to forget them. And they never did!

Cinderella's Friends ✓

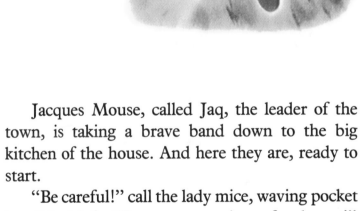

*T*weet! *Tweet!* It is morning. At the bluebird's song, Mouse Town, in the garret of Cinderella's house, wakes up with a squeak and a yawn.

Today is the day of the great Mouse Ball. Everyone is busy. The mice ladies are decking out the town. Even the bluebirds have come to help and join in the chorus of the merry mouse song. And this is what they sing:

> *"Cinderella, Cinderella,*
> *Is the sweetest one of all.*
> *Now she's marrying her prince, and*
> *So we're having a great ball!"*

Yes, the lady mice have the decorations well in hand. And the men are to provide the food.

Jacques Mouse, called Jaq, the leader of the town, is taking a brave band down to the big kitchen of the house. And here they are, ready to start.

"Be careful!" call the lady mice, waving pocket handkerchiefs. "Be sure to watch out for the cat!"

"We will!" the men promise. For they know that cat—the fat and evil Lucifer. But they are brave mice. Away they march, right through a hole in the wall.

Down, down, down dark tunnels they make their way. And as they march they sing a song:

> *"Cinderella, Cinderella,*
> *Is the princess of the land,*
> *And to make her ball a fine one,*
> *We will lend a helping hand."*

At last they stop. They have come to the kitchen of the house. "Sh!" says Jaq. And the song breaks off as Jaq creeps out for a look around.

There, in the coziest spot of all, close to the fire, lies Lucifer Cat. But he is fast asleep.

"Come on!" Jaq signals. And out they creep.

Here come the mice, all set for a climb. One, two, three, up to the chair. Four, five, six, to the tabletop. And they load themselves down with as much food as they can hold.

Then six, five, four, to the kitchen floor, and back, back, back toward the hole they go. But plump and greedy Gus spies one more piece of cheese. He can't pass it up. He reaches, and *snap*! Gus finds himself tight in a mousetrap.

Snap! Lucifer awakes! He opens one eye. The mice have vanished, all but Gus.

"Aha!" he snarls. "I've got you now!" And he springs!

"Hurry, men!" cries Jaq. "Into the wall!" The mice race for the wall, carrying what they can. Jaq stays behind to manage Lucifer. And he leads the cat a merry chase.

"Aha!" purrs Lucifer, with a horrid, hungry smile. He reaches out a paw, but it is not long enough.

"Ho-hum," yawns Lucifer to himself. "Someone will come soon and open the trap. I can have my feast then. I'll finish my nap."

"Zzzzzz," snores Lucifer Cat. And out from their hiding places all around, hush-hush-hush, creep the mice.

They shake their heads at greedy Gus. But one, two, three, they spring that trap!

And out comes Gus with a *ping*!

Ping! Up wakes Lucifer, and there are the mice.

Into the hole in the wall they climb, one, two, three—mouse after mouse with loads of food.

Now it's Gus's turn, with his grapes piled high. But he has too many. *Plink, plunk, scatter,* down they fall!

Poor Jaq. He is wearing out. Lucifer is coming close. Gus sees his friend's danger. But what can he do?

Squish! He steps on a grape. It hits Lucifer in the eye. While he screeches with rage—*zip!*—up go Jaq and Gus.

Then up, up, up through the walls they go, a happy band of mice. As they climb they sing a happy song. And this is the song they sing:

"Cinderella,
*   Cinderella,*
How we'll celebrate
*   tonight!*
We will feast and dance
*   and frolic*
By the moon and
*   candlelight!"*

And they did! You have never seen such a beautiful place as Mouse Town was that night. There has never been a more wonderful feast, with dancing and singing and cheering.

And that's how Cinderella's mice celebrated her wedding to the prince.

Mickey Mouse
Those Were the Days

"Hurry, Uncle Mickey, we're late!" cried Morty.

"We're not late," said Mickey. "The sun isn't even up yet."

"But Mr. Bumbles is up," said Ferdie.

He pointed to a sign that read "Founders' Village," a landmark that showed what life was like in the olden days. There stood Mr. Bumbles, the caretaker, with his suitcase and his train ticket. He was all ready to leave on his vacation.

Morty and Ferdie ran to say good-bye to Mr. Bumbles. Mickey and the boys were to be the caretakers of Founders' Village while Mr. Bumbles was away.

"We know just what to do!" said Morty. "Every morning the horse gets hitched to the surrey. Then when all the people come, we'll take them for a surrey ride around the village."

"Afterward we'll serve homemade lemonade and popcorn," Ferdie said. "We'll make the popcorn on the wood-burning stove."

"Sounds like you have it down pat," said Mr. Bumbles.

A taxi came up the hill, and Mr. Bumbles got in and sped away.

"Won't this be fun!" cried Ferdie. "A whole week living just the way our grandparents did."

"Those were the days, huh?" Morty chuckled as they started for the stable to hitch up the horse.

The horse had other ideas. It would not go near the surrey, and it would not stand still. The horse pranced and stamped and reared. The boys scampered and prodded and pleaded, but they could not get the harness on the animal.

Mickey tried to help the boys. The horse made a snorting, whinnying noise at him. Then it trotted into the stable and wouldn't come out again.

Morty sighed. "Maybe nobody will want a surrey ride today," he said. "Maybe if we give people lots of lemonade and popcorn, they won't even remember we have a surrey."

"We can hope," said Mickey, but he didn't sound too hopeful.

Mickey and the boys went to the kitchen to start on the lemonade. Instead of a faucet, they found a pump for water. Mickey pumped the handle up and down, up and down. The pump rattled and squealed and squeaked, but not a drop of water came out.

Morty searched the cupboards. "Where's the juicer?" he cried. "And where's the outlet to plug in the juicer? We can't squeeze lemons without a juicer."

"We can't serve lemonade without ice, either," said Ferdie. "There are no ice cubes in this refrigerator."

"It's not a refrigerator," said Mickey. "It's an icebox, and it's empty. I'll go to town later and buy some ice," said Mickey.

"Could you buy some wood, too?" asked Morty. "The woodbox is empty."

"There's a woodpile behind the stable," said Mickey. "You know what that means?"

"Does it mean we're supposed to chop big pieces of wood into little pieces?" asked Ferdie.

Mickey grinned. "You're living in the good old days now, and in those days boys chopped wood."

The boys sighed, but they chopped the wood. Then Mickey made a fire in the old stove.

For about three minutes the small fire burned brightly. Then smoke began to billow out into the kitchen.

"Uncle Mickey, the stove's on fire!" yelled Morty.

Mickey opened the stove lid. "Water!" he shouted. "Get water! I'll put it out!"

But there was no water. The pump didn't work.

Ferdie coughed and choked. He pulled the front door open. "I'll call the fire department!" he yelled.

He ran around Founders' Village, looking for a telephone, but there was none to be found. In the good old days people didn't have telephones.

By the time Ferdie got back to the house, the fire had died down. Mickey had thrown baking soda on the fire to put it out.

"That does it," said Mickey. "You two air out the kitchen. I'm going to town."

Mickey drove away toward town. When he came back, he had ice for the icebox.

"I made a couple of phone calls in town," Mickey told the boys. "Help is on the way."

Before long there was a rattling, clanking, chugging, puffing sound on the road. It was Goofy speeding to the rescue in his old car.

Minnie Mouse was with Goofy. So were Horace Horsecollar and Clarabelle Cow.

Clarabelle had once lived in the country, so she knew about wood-burning stoves. She turned a handle on the stovepipe. "That opens the draft," she said. "Now the stovepipe is clear and the smoke can go up the chimney."

Sure enough, when Mickey started a new fire in the stove, not a puff of smoke came out into the kitchen. Clarabelle started popping corn.

Minnie had never lived in the country, but she knew that lemonade was invented before people knew about electricity. She opened a cupboard and took out a funny-looking gadget.

"My grandma had a hand juicer, and it worked just fine," Minnie said. "This one should work, too. Ferdie, cut some lemons."

Ferdie did, and Minnie squeezed them on the hand juicer.

Horace Horsecollar fiddled with the pump. "I don't think it's broken," he said. "It just needs to be primed with water. It's a lucky thing I brought some water, just in case."

Horace carried a pail in from the car. He poured water from the pail into the pump. Then he moved the pump handle up and down.

This time the pump did not make an empty, rattling, squeaking sound. This time the pump gushed water.

"Great!" cried Ferdie. "Now we'll be all set if somebody can figure out an easy way to chop some more wood."

"No problem," said Horace. He led Morty and Ferdie out to the woodpile.

A car was pulling into a parking spot near the stable. A mother and father were in the front seat of the car, and two kids were in the backseat.

"Start chopping," Horace told the boys. "And smile! You love to chop wood! You're having a great time!"

"You've got to be kidding!" said Morty. But he and Ferdie began to chop the wood with huge grins on their faces. They even laughed out loud now and then as they worked.

The kids from the car wandered over to see what was happening. After they watched for a minute, one of them said, "Hey, Dad, can I chop some wood?"

"You can if you promise to be very careful," said the father. "I'll stand here and watch."

"Oh, maybe you'd better not," said Morty.

"It's really hard work," added Ferdie.

But the kids begged and pleaded. Soon Morty and Ferdie gave up their axes and let the visitors chop the wood.

"Pretty smart, aren't you?" said Morty to Horace. "Maybe you know how we can hitch the horse to the surrey."

But Goofy was tending to the horse. He led the horse out of the stable, and he whispered something in the horse's ear.

The horse gave a startled snort. Then it backed up to the surrey and stood still, and Goofy hitched it up.

Presto! The surrey was ready for a load of passengers.

"What did you say to the horse?" gasped Ferdie.

"I told him if he wanted to lose his job, I could fix it for him," said Goofy. "I said that my jalopy is as old as anything in Founders' Village, but it will start easier than a stubborn horse, and people love to ride in it."

The rest of the day was grand.

The rest of the week was even better, with surrey rides and fresh lemonade and hot popcorn for everyone.

"The olden days really were good, weren't they?" said Ferdie.

"You bet," said Mickey. "But with good friends, any day is good."

Donald Duck's Toy Sailboat

"There!" said Donald Duck. "At last it's done!"

He stood back to look at his toy sailboat. Making it had been a big job. It had taken him all summer long. But now the boat was finished. And it was a beautiful boat.

The mantel was just the place for it, too. The whole room looked better with the sailboat up there.

"Building sailboats is hungry work," Donald said to himself. So he fixed himself a fine big lunch.

"Now to try out the boat in the lake," he thought. But his hard work had made him sleepy, too. So Donald settled down for a nap after lunch.

Now, outside Donald's cottage in the old elm tree lived two little chipmunks, Chip 'n' Dale. And they had had no lunch at all.

"I'm hungry," said Chip, rubbing his empty middle.

"Me, too," said little Dale. But suddenly he brightened. "Look!" he said.

Chip looked and looked. At last he spied it—one lone acorn still clinging to the bough of an oak down beside the lake.

Down the elm tree they raced, across to the oak, and up its rough-barked trunk.

"Mine!" cried Chip, reaching for the nut.

"I saw it first!" Dale cried.

So they pushed and they tugged and they tussled, until the acorn slipped through their fingers and fell *kerplunk* into the lake.

The two little chipmunks looked mighty sad as they watched the acorn float away. But Dale soon brightened. "Look!" he cried.

Chip looked. On a little island out in the middle of the lake stood a great big oak tree weighted down with acorns on every side.

On the mantel in Donald Duck's cottage they could see the toy sailboat.

"Come on," said Dale. So away they raced.

They had the sailboat down and almost out the door when Donald stirred in his sleep.

"Nice day for a sail," he said dreamily as the boat slipped smoothly past his eyes.

Soon after, Donald woke up completely.

"Now to try out my boat!" he cried.

Suddenly something outside the window caught his eye. It was his sailboat, out on the lake!

"I'll fix those chipmunks!" Donald said.

He pulled out his fishing rod and reel and chose a painted lure. It looked just like a nut.

"This will do," Donald said, grinning.

From the pier, he cast that little fishing lure as far as he could. With a *plop* it landed beside the toy boat.

"Look! Look at this!" cried Dale. He leaned way over the edge of the boat to pull in the floating lure.

"Good! A nut!" said Chip. "We'll toss it in the hold and have it for supper tonight."

Down to the shore the chipmunks ran. But *br-r-r!* It was too cold to swim.

"How can we get to them?" wondered Chip.

"I don't know," said Dale. But he soon had an idea. "Look in there!" he said.

As soon as it was fast in the hold, Donald pulled in the line. He pulled that little boat right into shore. The chipmunks never suspected a thing. They did not even notice Donald pouring water into the cabin of the boat.

Chip discovered that when he went into the cabin. "Man the pumps!" he cried.

Those two chipmunks worked with might and main while Donald watched and laughed.

"Ha, ha!" At Donald's chuckle, the chipmunks looked up.

"So that's the trouble!" Dale cried.

He pulled out the fishing lure from the hold and flung it at Donald so that he was soon tangled up in fishing line.

While Donald tried to tug himself free the chipmunks set sail once more.

Before Donald could launch his swift canoe, they had touched the island's shore.

As Donald was paddling briskly along he heard a brisk *rat-a-tat-tat*!

The oak tree on the island seemed to shiver and shake as its store of acorns rained down. The busy little chipmunks finished dancing on the branches. Then they hurled their harvest on board.

"Oh, well," said Donald, watching from his canoe. "At least I know the sailboat really will sail. Now, let's just see what those little fellows do."

And can you guess what the chipmunks did? They stored their nuts in a hollow tree. And they took Donald's toy sailboat right back and put it where it belonged!

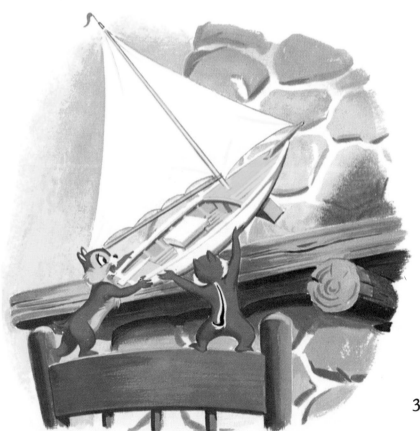

Winnie the Pooh
and the
Honey Patch

It was a fine spring morning when Owl and Pooh decided to take a walk. Owl ruffled his feathers in the warm air.

"The atmospheric conditions..." he began.

"Indeed," Pooh said.

Owl went on, "...and the prevailing winds mean that it is now time for—"

"Honey," Pooh interrupted.

"Honey?" said Owl impatiently. "Pooh, you are a bear of little brain and too much tummy. I was talking about *spring*! Spring is the time of the year when everything starts growing."

"I should say it's also a good time for someone to eat honey," Pooh replied. "Especially me."

Owl continued, speaking more loudly, "Spring is the time for Rabbit to plant carrot seeds, and for Piglet to plant small cabbage plants. Then they can eat carrots and cabbages all year long."

"All year long?" Pooh repeated. He had a lovely thought. "Owl, do you suppose that if I plant one of my honey pots, it will grow honey?"

"That sounds like a practical idea," Owl said. "But, then again, maybe it isn't. You see, Pooh—"

But Pooh wasn't listening. He was too busy thinking about a whole year's supply of honey in his very own honey patch.

That afternoon, Rabbit strolled past Pooh's house and heard him inside, pondering. "This big one? That small one? I shouldn't waste the big one—but a small one wouldn't grow much honey. Maybe I'll plant a middle-sized one."

"What are you planting?" Rabbit asked.

"Owl has given me a practical idea," Pooh explained. "I shall grow honey from a honey pot."

"This *is* a practical idea," Rabbit replied. "I'll help you with it."

So the two friends planted one middle-sized pot deep in the ground.

Before long, Rabbit's carrots poked through the ground, and Piglet's cabbage plants looked bigger. Pooh's honey pot, however, wasn't growing anything at all.

"Poor Pooh! I can't understand what's wrong," Rabbit told Piglet and Eeyore. "Maybe we should talk to Owl. He knows the scientifics about growing."

But when they asked Owl what was wrong, he ruffled his feathers and looked cross. "It wasn't *my* idea to grow honey from a pot! It was Pooh's idea!" he exclaimed. "Actually, I wondered from the beginning if it was a practical idea."

"Poor Pooh!" sighed Rabbit.

"Maybe we can *make* it work," Piglet squeaked in a very excited voice. "When Pooh is sleeping, we can dig up the honey pot. Perhaps if you look at it, Owl, you'll see what is wrong."

"I don't think—" Owl began. But they all looked at him so hopefully that he stopped right there.

That night, they crept carefully to the edge of Pooh's honey patch.

Rabbit whispered, "I think a very small animal should dig up a honey pot."

"Me?" Piglet squealed softly.

"Unless you're afraid," Rabbit replied.

Piglet marched bravely into the patch and began to dig. The deeper he went, the more the hole seemed like a place where a very large animal might come to rest in the dark.

Thump. He struck something hard.

He pulled and tugged. Suddenly the honey pot came free, and Piglet tumbled over backward.

"Help!" cried Piglet, thinking a whole herd of very large animals was upon him.

"Look! The pot's broken," Eeyore said. "Now we'll never know what was wrong."

Somehow Owl felt better.

"We must find another pot," Rabbit said firmly.

"I don't have a pot, but I do have a bucket I can spare," said Piglet.

He hurried home, with all the others for

company, and they carried the bucket back to Pooh's honey patch.

"I think," said Owl, "that what *this* honey pot needs is sun and air and an occasional rain. Those are important for growing. We'll fill up the hole, and we'll see what happens."

That was what they did. And that was why there was a bucket in the honey patch when Pooh hurried out the next morning. He wanted to see if anything exciting might have happened during the night.

He stared at the bucket in astonishment. "Think, think, think," he said to himself. "My honey pot didn't grow honey, but it did grow a

bucket. A very fine bucket, too. And a bucket is most useful when it is filled with something sweet."

Off he stamped into the woods to find something sweet to put in his bucket. He made up this hum to keep him company:

"If a bear in the summer,
   Clankety, clinkety,
   Has a garden to sow,
   Clinkety, clankety,
   It's much better to sing,
   Clankety, clinkety,
   Than to wait for his honey to grow."

He wished Piglet were with him to sing the *clinkety's* and *clankety's*. Piglet would like that.

While Pooh was off collecting honey, Rabbit, Piglet, Eeyore, and Owl stopped by to see if the bucket had grown anything.

"It's gone!" Rabbit exclaimed. "First no honey, then no honey pot, and now no bucket."

"I knew it," said Eeyore gloomily. "I could have guessed that this would happen."

They were about to ask Owl what to do next when Pooh came out of the woods.

"Hurray!" shouted Pooh, hurrying toward his friends. "Company for breakfast!"

"Pooh!" Rabbit shouted back. "You've filled our bucket with honey. How wonderful!"

"*Your* bucket?" Pooh asked. "Well, you are welcome to share, of course, but I did find this bucket growing here in *my* honey patch. And the handle makes it very useful for honey-finding time."

The others smiled while Piglet explained exactly how the bucket happened to grow in the honey patch. And then the friends all sat down together for a breakfast of honey.

"It's delicious," Piglet said, "but honey is certainly easier to find than it is to grow, wouldn't you say, Pooh?"

"Indeed," said Pooh.

"I hope you've learned that growing honey in the garden is not a practical idea after all," said Owl. "Still, with my knowledge of the atmosphere and the prevailing winds..."

"Indeed," said Pooh again.

"...our spring planting has yielded quite a fine crop!" Owl concluded proudly.

"Indeed," Pooh said once more, and he licked the last of the honey off his paws.

The Three Little Pigs

Once upon a time there were three little pigs who went out into the big world to build their homes and seek their fortunes.

The first little pig did not like to work at all. He quickly built himself a house of straw.

Then off he danced down the road to see how his brothers were getting along.

The second little pig was building himself a house, too. He did not like to work any better than his brother, so he had decided to build a quick and easy house of sticks.

Soon it was finished, too. It was not a very strong little house, but at least the work was done. Now the second little pig was free to do what he liked.

What he liked to do was to play his fiddle and dance. So while the first little pig tooted his flute,

the second little pig sawed away on his fiddle, dancing as he played. And as he danced he sang:

> *"I built my house of sticks,*
> *I built my house of twigs.*
> *With a hey diddle-diddle*
> *I play on my fiddle*
> *And dance all kinds of jigs."*

Then off danced the two little pigs down the road together to see how their brother was getting along.

The third little pig was a sober little pig. He was building a house, too, but he was building his of bricks. He did not mind hard work, and he wanted a stout little, strong little house, for he knew that in the woods nearby there lived a big bad wolf who liked nothing better than to catch little pigs and eat them up!

So *slap, slosh, slap!* Away he worked, laying bricks and smoothing mortar between them.

"Ha, ha, ha!" laughed the first little pig when he saw his brother hard at work.

"Ho, ho, ho!" laughed the second little pig. "Come down and play with us!" he called.

36

But the busy little pig did not pause. *Slap, slosh, slap!* went the bricks on mortar as he called down to them:

> *"I build my house of stones.*
> *I build my house of bricks.*
> *I have no chance*
> *To sing and dance,*
> *For work and play don't mix."*

"Ho, ho, ho! Ha, ha, ha!" laughed the two lazy little pigs, dancing along to the tune of the fiddle and the flute.

"You can laugh and dance and sing," their busy brother called after them, "but I'll be safe and you'll be sorry when the wolf comes to the door!"

"Ha, ha, ha! Ho, ho, ho!" laughed the two little pigs again, and they disappeared into the woods, singing a merry tune:

> *"Who's afraid of the big bad wolf,*
> *The big bad wolf, the big bad wolf?*
> *Who's afraid of the big bad wolf?*
> *Tra la la la la-a-a-a!"*

Just as the first pig reached his door, out of the woods popped the big bad wolf!

The little pig squealed with fright and slammed the door.

"Little pig, little pig, let me come in!" cried the wolf.

"Not by the hair of my chinny-chin-chin!" said the little pig.

"Then I'll huff, and I'll puff, and I'll blow your house in!" roared the wolf.

And he did. He blew the little straw house all to pieces!

Away raced the little pig to his brother's house of sticks. No sooner was he in the door when—knock, knock, knock—there was the big bad wolf!

But, of course, the little pigs would not let him come in.

"I'll fool those little pigs," said the big bad wolf to himself. He left the little pig's house, and he hid behind a big tree.

"Who's afraid of the big bad wolf,
The big bad wolf, the big bad wolf?
Who's afraid of the big bad wolf?
Tra la la la la-a-a-a!"

Soon there came another knock at the door. It was the big bad wolf again, but he had covered himself with a sheepskin and was curled up in a big basket, looking like a little lamb.

"Who's there?" called the second little pig.

Soon the door opened and the two little pigs peeked out. There was no wolf in sight.

"Ha, ha, ha! Ho, ho, ho!" laughed the two little pigs. "We fooled him."

Then they danced around the room, singing gaily:

"I'm a poor little sheep with no place to sleep. Please open the door and let me in," said the big bad wolf in a sweet little voice.

The second little pig peeked through a crack in the door, and he could see the wolf's big black paws and sharp fangs.

38

Soon the other two little pigs were singing and dancing with him.

This made the big bad wolf perfectly furious!

"Now by the hair of my chinny-chin-chin!" he roared, "I'll huff, and I'll puff, and I'll blow your house in!"

"Not by the hair of my chinny-chin-chin!" he said.

"You can't fool us with that sheepskin!" said the first little pig.

"Then I'll huff, and I'll puff, and I'll blow your house in!" cried the angry old wolf.

So he huffed, and he *puffed,* and he PUFFED, and he HUFFED, and he blew the little twig house all to pieces!

So the big bad wolf huffed,
and he *puffed,*
and he PUFFED,
and he HUFFED,

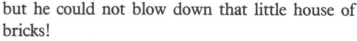

but he could not blow down that little house of bricks!

Then he huffed and puffed some more, and he shook the little door until it rattled, but the three little pigs inside only laughed and danced and sang still more merrily.

Away raced the two little pigs, straight to the third little pig's house of bricks.

"Don't worry," said the third little pig to his two frightened brothers. "You are safe here."

He began to sing and dance.

That made the wolf angrier than ever! He could not blow the house down, or shake the door loose, or pry open a window. How could he get in? At last he thought of the chimney!

Very quietly the big bad wolf climbed up onto the roof of the little brick house and sneaked over to the chimney.

The little pigs inside were worried because the wolf was so silent. They knew he must be up to something. Then they heard a rattling in the chimney, and they knew the big bad wolf was planning to come down that way and eat them up!

The third little pig rushed over to the fireplace and snatched the lid off the great pot of water boiling there.

Down came the wolf, into the hot water!

With a yelp of pain he sprang straight up the chimney again and raced away from that little house as fast as he could go!

The three little pigs saw him disappear into the deep woods, and they laughed and laughed and laughed. Then the little brick house rang with the tinkle of the piano and the toot of the flute and the sound of the fiddle as the three little pigs played and danced and sang:

"Who's afraid of the big bad wolf,
The big bad wolf, the big bad wolf?
Who's afraid of the big bad wolf?
Tra la la la la-a-a-a!"

But the big bad wolf did not hear them. He was hiding in his hole, deep in the woods. And he never came back again.

Dumbo

were just plain ridiculous. The audience sneered at him, and the other elephants scorned him.

Those big ears kept getting poor Dumbo into big trouble. The first time Dumbo lined up in the circus parade with the other elephants, he tripped over his own ears. The other elephants did not think that was very funny!

Later, a bunch of bullies came to the circus. First they teased Dumbo. When they got tired of that, they began to pinch and poke him. When one of the boys pulled his tail—hard!—Dumbo couldn't help but yell.

Dumbo, Mrs. Jumbo's baby boy, was the littlest elephant in the whole circus. He had a cute little trunk, a short little tail, and two of the biggest, floppiest ears ever.

Mrs. Jumbo thought everything about her son was just perfect. But everyone else thought his ears

Dumbo's mother ran to the rescue and gave that bully the spanking he deserved.

The bully cried, "Help! Help! Wild elephant!" The audience panicked and raced for the exits. Circus guards surrounded Mrs. Jumbo and tied her up.

"Put that beast in the prison car before she tramples all our customers," the ringmaster ordered. So the guards threw poor Mrs. Jumbo into a locked cage.

Without his mother to protect him, Dumbo's life was harder than ever. The other elephants blamed Dumbo's big ears for giving them and Mrs. Jumbo a bad name.

eyes. Timothy took care of that. "We'll just tie your ears in a knot," he said. "That should keep them out of your way."

All went well until the first show. Dumbo's heart was pounding as he ran into the center ring. Suddenly Dumbo's ears came undone, and he tripped over them, flying right into the teetering pyramid of elephants. *Crash! Smash!* All the elephants came tumbling down.

The elephants were furious. They declared that Dumbo was no longer one of them.

Luckily Timothy Q. Mouse believed that the other elephants were wrong about Dumbo. Timothy decided to be Dumbo's friend. He would try to help Dumbo prove he was a good elephant.

One day the ringmaster decided to put Dumbo in a brand-new act, the Great Pyramid. After the other elephants had formed a big pyramid, Dumbo would leap off a springboard and land on its very top.

Dumbo practiced long and hard. But no matter what he did, his floppy ears kept falling over his

The ringmaster was so angry that he threatened to send Dumbo to a zoo. But when he calmed down a bit, he decided instead to make Dumbo a clown. After all, the ringmaster thought, the funny-looking elephant would surely be able to make people laugh.

The clowns made Dumbo the butt of all their jokes. They set off firecrackers under his feet and threw pies in his face. They tripped him and teased him. To top it off, they decided to dress Dumbo like a baby and make him jump out of a fake burning building.

Dumbo soon found himself trembling on top of the fake building, while fake fire fighters clowned below. Too scared to jump, Dumbo felt the hot flames at his feet. Then he felt a shove from behind as one of the clowns pushed him out of the open window. Down, down Dumbo fell—through the fire fighters' safety net and into a tub of mud.

The audience laughed and laughed, but Dumbo felt like crying. To cheer him up, Timothy suggested that they visit Mrs. Jumbo. Late that night the two pals sneaked over to the prison car. Mrs. Jumbo stuck her trunk out through the bars and gave her boy a big hug.

"Don't let the hard times get you down," she told Dumbo. "Just do your best, and someday you'll be flying high."

By the time Dumbo left his mother, he was feeling much better. With Timothy tucked snugly into his cap, Dumbo strolled into the countryside. He began to hop and then to dance. Far into the night Dumbo frolicked in the moonlight.

The next thing Timothy knew, it was morning. He was surprised to find that he and Dumbo weren't in their circus tent, or even on the ground. They were perched on a high branch of a very tall tree. And they weren't alone. On a nearby branch sat a whole flock of crows.

When Dumbo woke up, he was surprised, too. He fell right out of the tree and into a shallow pond.

"I wonder how we ever got up there," Timothy said.

"There's only one way up," the biggest crow said. "You must have flown."

"But we don't know how to fly," Timothy protested.

"It's easy," the crow replied. "Just flap your wings." The bird pointed to Dumbo's big ears.

Timothy thought flying could be Dumbo's chance to prove he was a star elephant. But Dumbo didn't remember flying, and he didn't think he could do it again.

"If you need a little help," a crow said, "take this." He handed Dumbo a shiny black feather. "It's magic," the crow explained. "Hold on to this and you can't help but fly."

Dumbo took the magic feather in his trunk and began to flap his ears.

Faster and faster Dumbo flapped, but his feet remained planted firmly on the ground.

"Come on, Dumbo," Timothy urged. "You just need to get a good start." Timothy and the crows led Dumbo up to a high ledge. The little elephant again began flapping his ears, and the crows gave him a gentle push.

Suddenly Dumbo was in the air. At first he was scared, and he almost crashed. But then he remembered his magic feather. He spread his big ears and suddenly he was flying like a bird. He swooped and he soared. What fun it was to fly!

Dumbo was having a lot of fun. But suddenly the magic feather slipped from his trunk and fluttered to the ground. Dumbo panicked and began to plummet after it.

Dumbo would have crashed if he hadn't heard Timothy cry, "Come on, Dumbo. You don't need that feather to fly. All you need is your own two ears."

After thanking the crows, Dumbo and Timothy headed back to the circus. They got there just as Dumbo's act was about to begin. Once more Dumbo found himself atop a burning building. Once more he was pushed through the window. But this time it was Dumbo who had the last laugh, for instead of dropping like a stone into the net, he glided gracefully up into the air.

As the crowd gasped in amazement Dumbo flew higher and higher. Upside down, right side up—the happy little elephant flew every which way.

Dumbo knew his friend was right. Spreading his big ears, he hovered just inches from the ground. Then he gave a mighty flap, and soon he was flying higher than ever.

From that day on, Dumbo was a star. The ringmaster changed the name of the show to Dumbo's Flying Circus. Dumbo got all the peanuts he could eat, plus a private car on the circus train, where he could be with his mother.

All the other elephants tried to stretch their ears so they could be just like Dumbo. It was no use, for there never was and never would be but one flying elephant—Dumbo!

Bunny Book

Deep in the woods, where the brier bushes grow, lies Bunnyville, a busy little bunny rabbit town.

And in the very center of that busy little town stands a cottage—a neat twig cottage with a neat brown roof—that is known to all as the very own home of Great-Grandpa Bunny Bunny.

Great-Grandpa Bunny Bunny, as every bunny knows, was the ancestral founder of the town.

He liked to tell the young bunnies who always gathered around how he and Mrs. Bunny Bunny, when they were very young, had found that very brier patch and built themselves that very same little twig house.

It was a happy life they lived there, deep in the woods, bringing up their bunny family in that little house of twigs.

And of course Daddy Bunny Bunny, as he was called then, was busy at his job, decorating Easter eggs.

As the children grew up they helped paint Easter eggs. And soon they were all grown-up, with families of their own, and they built a ring of houses all around their parents' home.

By and by they had a town there, and they called it Bunnyville.

Now, Grandpa Bunny Bunny looked for other

jobs to do. He taught the young folk to paint flowers in the woods. They tried out new shades of green on mosses and ferns.

They made those woods so beautiful that people said, "The soil must be especially rich."

But the bunnies knew that it was all Grandpa Bunny Bunny's doing.

Years went by, and there were still more families in Bunnyville. And Grandpa Bunny Bunny had grown to be Great-Grandpa Bunny Bunny. He had so much help that he looked around for other jobs to do. He taught the bunnies to paint autumn leaves.

Through the woods they scampered with their brushes and pails. And people would say to themselves, "Never has there been so much color in these woods. The nights must be especially frosty hereabouts."

But the bunnies knew that it was all their great-grandpa's plan.

And so it went as the seasons rolled around. There were constantly more bunnies in that busy Bunnyville. And Great-Grandpa was busy finding jobs for them to do.

He taught them in winter to paint shadows on the snow, and pictures in frost on wintry windowpanes, and to polish up the diamond lights on glittering icicles.

And between times he told stories to each crop of bunny young, around the cozy fire in his neat little twig home. The bunny children loved him and his funny bunny tales. And they loved the new and different things he found for them to do.

And the bunnies wondered what he would think of next! Well, Great-Grandpa stayed at home a lot those days and thought and thought and thought.

And at last he told a secret to that season's bunny boys and girls.

"Children," Great-Grandpa Bunny Bunny said, "I am going to go away. And I'll tell you what my next job will be if you'll promise not to say."

But at last it did seem as if he'd thought of everything! He had crews of bunnies trained to paint the first tiny buds of spring.

He had teams who waited beside cocoons to touch up the wings of new butterflies.

Some specialized in beetles, some in creeping, crawling things.

They had painted up that whole wild wood till it sparkled and gleamed.

So the bunny children promised. And Great-Grandpa went away. The older bunnies missed him, and often they looked sad. But the bunny children only smiled and looked extremely wise. For they knew a secret they had promised not to tell.

Then one day a windy rainstorm pelted down on Bunnyville. Everyone scampered speedily home and stayed cozy and dry indoors.

After a while the rain slowed down to single dripping drops.

Then every front door opened, and out the bunny children ran.

"Oh, it's true!" those bunnies shouted. And they did a bunny dance. "Great-Grandpa's been at work again. Come see what he has done!"

And the people walking out that day looked up in pleased surprise.

"Have you ever," they cried, "simply *ever* seen a sunset so gorgeously bright!?"

The little bunnies heard them and they chuckled silently. For they knew that it was all Great-Grandpa Bunny Bunny's plan.

Donald Duck and the Witch

It was getting on toward Halloween. Donald Duck and his nephews were hunting for pumpkins for jack-o'-lanterns.

The day was almost over, and red and gold clouds were piling up in the sky, when they found a field that was full of pumpkins perfect for them.

They were walking back to the farmhouse, each with a round, ripe pumpkin in his arms, when Huey stopped them all with a shout.

"Look! A witch on a broomstick!" he cried.

They all saw a dark form streak across the sky.

"Pooh!" said Donald. "Witches, pooh! There are no witches, you know that. It must have been some sort of a bird you saw."

But the boys were not convinced.

Next day they set out to look for the witch.

They had a long, hard walk through the tangled woods. There was no path to follow, and they were not even sure just what they hoped to find.

At last they heard a cackling laugh up ahead. And what could be a surer sign of a witch than a crickling, cackling laugh?

"Sh!" said Dewey, with his fingers on his lips. And he led the way through the underbrush into the clearing beyond.

There stood a crooked little house, clearly the home of a witch. From the crooked little chimney rose a thread of smoke.

Smoke and steam rolled up in clouds from a cauldron out in front. And through the smoke came that merry, scary sound, the cackling laugh of a witch.

"Welcome, boys, welcome," said the witch's voice. "Welcome to Witch Hazel's little home." Then she came hobbling toward them, a merry little sprite, grinning with witchery glee.

The boys were speechless with surprise.

"What can I do for you today?" Witch Hazel asked of them. "Any spells you'd like me to cast? Anybody you'd like to bewitch?" And she poked Louie in the ribs while she gave him a sly wink.

"Bewitch!" echoed Louie.

"Cast spells!" said Dewey.

"Uncle Donald!" cried Huey.

They all agreed. They told Witch Hazel how Donald refused to believe in witches.

"We'll show him!" she cackled, beckoning them close.

From the pockets of her dress she tossed bits of this and that into her steaming pot.

"A real witch's brew!" gasped Dewey as swirls of smoke in mysterious shapes began to rise and blow.

"We'll show that Donald!" Witch Hazel vowed. "You meet me here on Halloween."

Home went the boys, and they said not a word about their adventure to Donald Duck.

Donald was not surprised when the boys disappeared early on Halloween.

He was not surprised when his doorbell rang soon after dark that night. There beneath the porch light stood the boys. Donald chuckled as he recognized them through their disguises. They were dressed as witches, one and all.

"Come in," said Donald with a grin, holding his door open wide. They parked their broomsticks beside the door. Donald rubbed his eyes as he thought he saw one jump. That, he knew, could not have been.

In came the witches, one, two, three. No, there were one, two, three, four!

Donald was surprised, but he did not say a word as they all took seats around the room.

"Treats?" he asked, passing a tray of fancy little cakes.

"Ouch!" cried Dewey, who reached for one first. A mousetrap was stuck on his thumb.

"Wow!" cried Louie, who reached for one next. It turned out to be a jack-in-the-box.

"Glub!" gulped Huey when he bit into his. It was all made of rubber, you see.

"Thanks," said the fourth guest with a cackling laugh. She blew at her cake, and it exploded into dust, right in Donald's face.

"Serves you right, smartie," said a voice. Donald whirled around. There were only the jack-o'-lanterns sitting there, grinning saucily. But as Donald looked it seemed to him that the merry faces shook with glee.

"We must be leaving now," one witch said.

"Won't you come with us, and let us return your hospitality?"

"No, thanks," said Donald, clinging to the doorknob as they all swept him onto the porch.

It was four against one. He soon found himself astride a broomstick.

"Abracadabra, boys! Here we go!" he heard a voice cackle in his ear.

All around him he saw broomsticks fly—and to his horror Donald saw the ground sink away below him, too!

Over the treetops and straight toward the moon the broomstick pointed, then down to the woods.

"Welcome to Witch Hazel's little home," he heard the cackling voice say. And down tumbled Donald—down, down, down into the witch's pot!

"Ho, ho, ho!" laughed the other three. He knew his nephews' voices all too well.

Donald gasped and sputtered. And he sizzled with rage when they hauled him out, soaking wet to the skin.

The witches did not notice. They were all doubled over, shaking with laughter.

Witch Hazel disappeared into her little house and came back with an extra dress and a hat.

"Better put on something dry," she told Donald with a grin. And he stamped off into the house.

When he came out again, a table was set close beside the bubbling pot. Three jack-o'-lanterns glowed on a Halloween feast of pumpkin pie, apple tart, corn on the cob, and all sorts of delicious things.

"Have a real treat, Uncle Donald," the nephews said, lifting off their masks.

So they all sat down and ate their fill—yes, Witch Hazel, too.

After a while, even Donald could smile.

"I still don't believe in witches," he said to Witch Hazel with a courtly bow. "But if there were any, I'd want them to be just like you."

Mickey and the Beanstalk

Far, far away, where the trees were greener than the prettiest green and the sky was bluer than the brightest blue, there was a place called Happy Valley. In Happy Valley the brooks babbled, the birds sang, and everyone smiled all day long.

The farmers whistled and hummed as they did their chores. Children sang as they skipped to school. In Happy Valley every day was a happy day.

High on a hill overlooking Happy Valley stood a <u>magnificent</u> castle. In the castle was the Golden Harp, who sang all day and cast a magic spell of happiness over the land.

But one day a terrible thing happened in Happy Valley. Someone stole the Golden Harp from the castle, and the magic spell of happiness was gone.

The birds stopped singing. The brooks stopped <u>babbling</u>. The crops stopped growing. The cows stopped giving milk. And all the people of Happy Valley grew sad and hungry.

"We must do something," said Farmer Donald.

"We'll starve if we don't," added Farmer Goofy.

"I know!" said Farmer Mickey. "I'll sell Bossy the cow and buy some food."

Mickey took the cow into town and sold her. When he returned, he said, "I have sold Bossy for three wonderful beans."

"Three beans!" cried Donald and Goofy. "We can't live on three beans!" Donald threw the beans on the floor in disgust.

"But...but...they are magic beans," said Mickey as he sadly watched the beans roll through a crack in the floor.

But Goofy and Donald didn't pay any attention to what Mickey was saying. They were too tired and hungry to listen.

During the night a moonbeam shone through the window and through the crack in the floor onto the beans.

The beans sprouted and began to grow. They grew into a stalk that lifted the house. The beanstalk climbed all the way up to the sky.

In the morning the hungry farmers woke up and looked out the window.

To their surprise Happy Valley was gone! All they could see from their window was a <u>tremendous</u> castle.

"Let's go!" said Mickey. "Whoever lives in that big castle must have plenty of food to share!"

Mickey, Donald, and Goofy climbed up to the top of the castle stairs and crawled under the front door. On an enormous table they saw huge platters of food. Mammoth pitchers of fresh cold milk waited for them. The farmers quickly climbed up a table leg and ate, drank, and laughed merrily.

As they were finishing their meal a tiny voice called out to them.

"Who's that?" asked Mickey.

"It came from in there," said Donald, pointing to a box that was on the table.

Mickey, Donald, and Goofy moved closer to the box. "Who are you?" they asked.

"It is I, the Golden Harp," said a soft voice. "A giant kidnapped me and brought me here to his castle to sing for him."

The farmers were very frightened to hear that the castle belonged to a giant. They were so frightened that they almost ran away.

"Wait!" cried Mickey suddenly. "We can't leave without the Golden Harp."

"You're right," said Goofy bravely. "We have to rescue her and save Happy Valley!"

Just then, they heard loud footsteps. Everything in the room was shaking as the footsteps came closer and closer.

"You must hide!" cried the Golden Harp.

Mickey, Donald, and Goofy ran as quickly as they could to hide from the evil giant.

The giant stomped over to the table and picked up a giant sandwich in his giant hand. He was just about to take a bite when he noticed that the sandwich was moving.

"There's a mouse in my sandwich!" roared the giant.

"Oh, I'm sorry," said Mickey. "I had no idea this was your sandwich." He jumped from the sandwich to the giant's shirt and then slid down the giant's leg.

"Run!" shouted Mickey to Donald and Goofy.

The giant was furious. He chased the three farmers around the room until they were cornered. The giant reached down to scoop them up in his hand—but he missed Mickey!

The great big giant put the tiny little farmers into the box with the Golden Harp. He locked the box and slipped the key into his great big pocket. Then he sat down in a chair to take a nap.

Mickey waited in his hiding place behind the pitcher. When the giant finally fell asleep, Mickey tiptoed over to the box and knocked.

"The key," whispered the Golden Harp. "Get the key out of his pocket."

Mickey hurried over to the sleeping giant. Very slowly and carefully he pulled the key out of the giant's pocket.

The giant mumbled something and stirred, but he did not wake up.

Mickey tiptoed back to the box and unlocked it. Goofy and Donald climbed out and then quickly lifted out the Golden Harp. The four were very quiet as they made their way to the front door.

Just as they were sneaking past the giant, he opened one eye and let out a giant roar.

Goofy and Donald ran with the Golden Harp in their arms. Mickey realized the giant would catch them unless he could do something to distract him.

"You can't catch me!" Mickey taunted. The angry giant ran toward Mickey, who dived under a rug. "Over here!" Mickey said, but the giant was not fast enough to catch him.

Mickey ran toward an open window. "So long!" he shouted as he jumped outside.

Mickey ran to the beanstalk with the giant following close behind. He jumped onto the beanstalk and slid down in a flash.

Donald and Goofy grabbed a saw and cut down the beanstalk in the nick of time. The giant fell and crashed through the ground, all the way to the center of the earth.

The farmers took the Golden Harp back to her castle to sing, and from that time on, Happy Valley was happy once again. And happiest of all were the three brave farmers—Mickey, Donald, and Goofy!

Bambi

One spring morning, in a little hidden forest glade, a fawn was born. All the birds and animals came to see him, for he was a very special fawn.

"What will you name the young prince?" asked Thumper the rabbit.

"I will call him Bambi," the mother answered.

The forest was filled with friends. The opossums and squirrels and robins and wrens all said, "Hello, young prince!" when Bambi walked down the leafy paths with his mother. And Thumper and Flower the skunk came out to play with Bambi nearly every day.

One morning Bambi's mother took him down a path where he had never been. At the end of the path was a wide green meadow.

What a wonderful place the meadow was! There was so much room to run and jump. Bambi leapt into the air three, four, five times.

When he stopped to catch his breath, another fawn came up to him. "Hello," she said softly.

Bambi tried to hide behind his mother.

"Don't be afraid, Bambi," she said. "This is Faline. Her mother is your aunt Ena."

Soon Bambi and Faline were racing around the meadow together.

Suddenly they heard hoofbeats. A herd of stags came galloping across the meadow, led by the great prince of the forest.

The great prince was older and bigger and stronger than the other stags, and he was very brave and wise. He said just one word: "MAN!"

All the birds and animals followed him back into the woods. Bambi was at his side. They heard frightening roaring noises behind them as they ran.

Later, when Bambi and his mother were safely back in their thicket, his mother explained.

"That was man in the meadow, Bambi. He brings danger and death to the forest with his long stick that roars and spurts flames. Someday you will understand."

The months passed, and the days grew cool. Winter was coming.

One morning when Bambi woke up, everything was covered with white.

"It's snow," his mother said. "Go ahead and walk on it."

Bambi stepped out and saw Thumper sliding on the frozen pond.

"Come on," Thumper called. "The water's *stiff*!"

Bambi trotted onto the ice. His front legs shot forward, his rear legs slipped back, and down he crashed!

"That's okay," said Thumper, laughing. "We can play something else. Winter's fun!"

But winter was also a hard time for the forest animals. Food was scarce. Sometimes Bambi and his mother had nothing to eat but the bark on the trees.

One day, when it seemed there was no food left anywhere, Bambi's mother found a few pale blades of grass growing under the snow.

They were nibbling the grass when they suddenly smelled man. As they lifted their heads they heard a deafening roar.

"Quick," said Bambi's mother, "run for the thicket."

Bambi darted away. He heard his mother's hoofbeats behind him, then another roar from man's guns. Terrified, he ran faster.

When Bambi reached the thicket, his mother was nowhere in sight. He sniffed for her scent. There was nothing.

"Mother!" he called, racing wildly out into the forest. "Mother, where are you?"

The great prince of the forest appeared beside him.

"Your mother can't be with you anymore," the prince said. "You must learn to walk alone."

Bambi did not understand, but he knew he must listen to the great prince. In silence he followed the old stag through the snowy forest.

At last spring arrived. The forest was turning green and leafy. And Bambi was growing into a handsome buck.

One day Bambi met a beautiful, graceful doe in the woods. "Hello," he said. "Who are you?"

"Don't you remember me?" the doe asked. "I'm Faline." Gently she licked Bambi's face.

Suddenly Ronno, a buck with big antlers, pushed his way between them. He began to nudge Faline down the path.

"Faline is coming with me," he said.

Bambi charged forward and butted Ronno with all his might. Again and again he and Ronno

crashed into one another, forehead to forehead.

A prong broke from one of Ronno's antlers, and he lost his balance. He fell to the ground, hurting his shoulder.

Ronno limped off by himself, and Bambi and Faline walked down the path together.

That night Bambi and Faline went out to the meadow and stood in the moonlight, listening to the east wind and the west wind calling to each other.

One morning in autumn Bambi sniffed the scent of man again. As he ran to warn Faline he smelled something else, too—smoke.

The old prince came and said, "The forest has caught fire from the flames of man's campfires. We must go to the river."

Bambi turned to Faline. "Run!" he said. "Run to the river." Faline raced off as Bambi and the prince ran to warn the other animals.

At last Bambi and the prince struggled across the rushing river. When they were safely on the other side, Faline came running to Bambi. They stood with the other animals on the bank and watched the flames destroy their forest home.

"When the forest is green again, I will be very old," said the prince. "Bambi, you must take my place then."

Bambi bowed his head.

When spring came, green leaves and grass and flowers covered the scars left by the fire.

At the thicket, the squirrels and rabbits and birds were peering through the undergrowth at Faline and two spotted fawns.

And not far away was Bambi, the proud father and the new great prince of the forest.

Thumper

In a forest high in the hills lived many animals. There were opossums and foxes, squirrels and mice. Bambi the young deer lived there, and so did Flower the skunk. There were many birds, too, and the wisest of them all was the owl.

But the largest family in the woods was the rabbit family. The mother rabbit had five children, and they kept her busy indeed.

There was Blossom, who had tall, beautiful ears.

There was Frilly, who was very playful. She would rather play than eat or sleep.

There was Violet, who had a bushy tail and was very shy.

There was Milly, who was always so hungry that she could never get enough to eat.

And there was Thumper.

Training a big family of rabbits is not easy, but the mother rabbit found most of her children to be very good. Of course, she wished that Milly would not eat *quite* so much, and she hoped that Violet would stop being so terribly shy. But they were all good about learning manners and obeying.

All except Thumper.

Sweet as he looked, he was a problem!

Every morning the rabbit family went to the meadow and played in the tall grass. Then they went over to a big patch of clover to eat their breakfast.

One day the mother rabbit was watching her children eat breakfast.

"Blossom, come back here and finish your meal," she called. Instead of eating, Blossom was looking into the pond, admiring the reflection of her beautiful big ears.

Frilly was playing, as usual. "Frilly, you mustn't play with that butterfly until you've eaten two more clumps of greenery," she cried.

Then the mother rabbit noticed Thumper. Nibbling at some sweet flowers, Thumper was not even touching the green leaves.

"Thumper! The flowers are for dessert. What did the wise old owl tell you about eating the leaves first?"

Thumper hung his head, looked at the ground, and thumped his left rear foot. Then he recited what the owl had told him:

> *"Eating greens is a special treat.*
> *They make long ears and great big feet.*

"But it sure is awful stuff to eat," he added to himself in a whisper.

Thumper's mother wanted him to eat properly, but *that* was not what worried her most. In the beautiful meadow, she could always make sure that all of her children ate enough greens.

What worried her most about Thumper was...his THUMPING!

Now, all of her children thumped once in a while, beating their strong rear feet against the ground. Rabbits are supposed to thump sometimes, especially when there is danger.

But Thumper thumped about everything.

He thumped when he was ashamed!

He thumped when he was hungry!

He thumped when he was angry!

And he thumped when he was happy!

Thumper really liked to thump.

But Thumper's sisters and Thumper's mother did *not* like his thumping.

"I just can't seem to help it," explained Thumper. "When something happens, I just have to thump."

One day, when the rabbit family was getting ready to go to the meadow, Thumper thumped loudly in his excitement.

"Now, this just *has* to stop!" cried his mother. "I'll have to punish you. Today you cannot go to the meadow with us. Just stay here alone, and maybe you'll learn to control that thumping."

Thumper watched his mother and his sisters hop away. He thumped a few thumps because he was lonely, but then he thought of his friend the owl.

At the base of the tall oak where the big bird had his nest, Thumper thumped as loudly as he could and called, "Hello, Friend Owl."

But Thumper had forgotten that it was daylight and the owl would be sound asleep.

"Stop that infernal noise!" growled the owl, yawning. "What do you mean by waking me out of a sound sleep? If you don't stop that thumping, young man, you're going to get into trouble. Now go away!"

Thumper was very sad. Even the old owl, who had always been his best friend, was angry with him.

The only thing to do, he decided, was to run away from home. Maybe somewhere else he would find friends who didn't mind his thumping.

So Thumper set off, hopping in the opposite direction from the meadow. He had never been very far that way, because his mother had told him it was dangerous. Man, who hunted in the forest with his big hunting dogs, lived there.

Thumper didn't know anything about man or the dogs, except that all the animals said they were dangerous. But maybe they wouldn't care if he thumped!

After a few minutes Thumper suddenly heard a strange sound ahead of him. He stopped and listened. Something was crashing through the forest toward him!

Thumper was frightened, so of course he thumped on the ground. The hunting dogs heard the thump and came running toward Thumper. And behind the dogs came the hunters!

Racing homeward, Thumper saw a hollow log and ran into it. He thumped and thumped and thumped, and the log boomed loudly.

Nearby, the frog was startled and leapt into the air. Then, when he heard the dogs barking around Thumper's hollow log, the frog was so frightened that he jumped into a nest of pheasants.

"The hunters are coming! Thumper the rabbit warned me!" cried the frog.

The pheasants flew to the oak and woke up the owl. The owl shouted to the crows, and all the birds called to the animals of the forest, "Man! The hunters are coming! Run to the hills for safety! Thumper the rabbit has given the warning!"

So the animals and the birds of the forest fled to the hills. The hunters and their dogs tramped through the forest for a long time, but all of the forest birds and animals had gotten away safely.

Finally, after several hours, the hunters went home, and the forest was quiet once more.

All the animals returned.

All but Thumper.

Thumper, very frightened by the hunters, still sat inside his hollow log.

The owl and the frog brought Thumper's mother to the log, and then Thumper came out.

The hunters were gone, but now Thumper was afraid his mother would punish him for running away from home. And, in fact, the mother rabbit was ready to scold her son for giving her such a fright.

But the frog and the owl told her how Thumper had warned them of the hunters.

"If it hadn't been for Thumper and his thumping," said the owl, "we would have been in terrible danger."

Then, instead of scolding Thumper, the mother rabbit beamed with pleasure. And as she took her little son home she vowed that she would never again scold him for thumping too much. All of the birds and animals of the forest agreed with her.

And now Thumper thumps whenever and wherever he likes!

Scamp

Lady was the mother.

Tramp was the father.

Their puppies were the finest ever.

They were sure of that.

Three were as gentle and as pretty as their mother.

But the fourth little puppy—

"Where is that puppy? Where is that Scamp?" they cried.

At mealtime three pretty little gentle puppies would line up, waiting for their bowl.

But the fourth little puppy, that Scamp of a puppy, would rush in ahead of them all.

At playtime three pretty little gentle puppies would play with their own puppy toys.

But the fourth little puppy, that Scamp of a puppy, would nibble at anything.

At bedtime three pretty little gentle puppies would snuggle down to sleep.

But the fourth little puppy, that Scamp of a puppy, chose that time to learn to howl, loud and long.

He found some new playmates.

Their game looked like fun.

But—*sss-ss-sst!*—they didn't want Scamp to play.

So Scamp got out of there.

He found another playmate.

It was a busy gopher, digging as fast as it could dig.

"Looks like fun," said Scamp. "How did you learn to do it?"

One day the four little puppies started off for a picnic with nice puppy biscuits for lunch.

Three little puppies went straight to the park and hunted for a shady spot.

But the fourth little puppy, that Scamp of a puppy, went off on an adventure.

"By digging," Mr. Gopher said. So Scamp dug, too.

He dug and dug and dug.

And what do you think he found?

A big, juicy bone.

It was a great big bone for a small dog.

Scamp pulled at it.

He tugged and hauled.

He tugged that bone all the way down the street to the park.

Just as Scamp got there, a big bad dog was saying, "Ha! I smell puppy biscuits."

So he sneaked up on those three little puppies and took their puppy-biscuit lunch.

Poor little puppies!

They were really very hungry. And they felt very sad.

Just then, who should appear but the fourth little puppy, that Scamp of a puppy, tugging his great big bone!

"Hi, folks," he said. "Look what I found. How about joining me?"

So they ate the big, juicy bone for lunch. And they all had a fine time.

When picnic time was over, those three pretty little gentle puppies all went happily home.

And the fourth little puppy, that Scamp of a puppy, walked proudly at the head of the line.

The Little Mermaid

Ariel's Underwater Adventure

An episode from the movie

Once upon a time there was a beautiful little mermaid named Ariel. She was the youngest daughter of the Sea King, Triton. Even though she lived at the bottom of the ocean, Ariel was not interested in her watery world. This little princess was only interested in the world above the ocean— the world of humans.

Ariel spent most of her time searching through sunken ships, looking for objects that had once belonged to humans. To Ariel these rusty old things were wonderful treasures.

One afternoon Ariel was treasure hunting in a graveyard of old sunken ships with her best friend, Flounder the fish.

"Come on, Flounder!" shouted Ariel as she swam into a broken-down ship. "Let's look in here."

"Are you sure it's safe?" asked Flounder.

"Sure," answered Ariel. "Follow me."

Inside, Ariel found a chest full of treasures.

"Oh, Flounder!" gasped Ariel. "Have you ever seen anything this wonderful in your entire life?"

Among the objects in the ship, Ariel found a fork and a pipe. "This is great!" the little mermaid cried. She put the objects into a pouch. "I don't have any of these in my collection yet!"

"Shark!" screamed Flounder as he raced back inside.

Ariel grabbed her bag of treasures. She and Flounder swam quickly to the upper deck. The shark followed, snapping his jaws. Ariel and Flounder squeezed through a porthole.

The small porthole didn't stop the shark. He crashed right through the side of the ship after them.

The mermaid and her little companion were swimming hard, but they were barely staying ahead of the shark's terrible jaws. The shark lunged at them, his jaws snapping the ship's mast as if it were a matchstick.

Just then Flounder heard a noise. "W-what was that?" he cried.

"I didn't hear anything," said Ariel, who was too busy looking for more treasures to notice any strange sounds.

Trembling with fear, Flounder peeked outside the doorway of the ship. There, with his huge mouthful of sharp teeth open wide, was a shark.

The two swam as fast as they could toward a huge old anchor. The shark followed, only inches behind them.

"I hope this works," gasped Ariel.

"M-me, too," cried Flounder.

When they reached the anchor, Ariel and Flounder slipped through the ring at the top. The shark tried to follow, but he was too big. His enormous face got stuck in the anchor.

"Let's get out of here," said Ariel. "We can head up to the surface to show Scuttle my new treasures."

On the surface, Ariel and Flounder visited with their friend Scuttle the sea gull. Ariel pulled one of her new treasures out of the pouch.

"Do you know what this is?" Ariel asked Scuttle, handing him the fork.

"Why, certainly," replied the cockeyed sea gull.

"After all, I'm the world's greatest expert on humans. This is a...a dingelhopper. Humans use it to straighten their hair, like this." Scuttle ran the old fork through Ariel's hair.

"What's this, Scuttle?" asked Ariel, this time handing him the pipe.

"This is most definitely a...a snarfblatt!" he answered. "It's used to make music." Scuttle blew into the pipe, but nothing came out except water. "Hmm. Nothing worse than a defective snarfblatt!"

Soon it was time for Ariel and Flounder to leave. They said good-bye to Scuttle and returned to the undersea kingdom.

Ariel went to her secret cave, where she hid all her human treasures.

The two friends were playing with Ariel's special collection when suddenly the cave got very dark. Ariel looked up through an opening and noticed something on the surface of the water blocking out the moonlight.

"I'm going to see what that is, Flounder," said Ariel.

On the ocean's surface was a very big ship.

"How beautiful it is!" exclaimed Ariel. "We've got to get a closer look."

Ariel reached up and peered over the side of the ship while Flounder looked on from the water below. Ariel saw a young man. His shipmates were singing and dancing.

"I've never seen a human this close before," said Ariel to Scuttle, who was also curious about the humans and had come for a better look.

"He's very handsome, isn't he?" said Ariel, looking at the young man the sailors called Prince Eric.

"He looks kind of hairy to me," said Scuttle, looking at Prince Eric's sheepdog, Max.

But Ariel didn't hear the sea gull. All she could think about was the young man—the one she would someday join in the world of humans. Ariel was falling in love.

Suddenly, without warning, a big storm came up. Rain poured down, lightning flashed, and the wind tossed the ship like a toy sailboat. Ariel watched Prince Eric as he and his crew tried to keep the ship afloat.

As the ship tossed and turned in the water a bolt of lightning hit the mast. The burning mast collapsed onto a keg of gunpowder. The explosion threw Prince Eric overboard into the raging waves.

"The prince!" shouted Ariel.

Prince Eric sank under the water. Ariel knew that if she didn't act at once, her handsome prince would drown.

Ariel dived into the sea. She grabbed Prince Eric and brought him up to the surface. Holding him tightly, she swam to shore and dragged the prince onto the sandy beach.

While the prince lay sleeping, Ariel stroked his hair and sang him a beautiful love song. How Ariel wished she could be with Prince Eric in the human world!

Before the prince began to stir, Ariel heard his crew coming. She knew she had to leave before she was seen by the humans.

Blowing the prince a kiss, Ariel turned and dived back into the ocean.

Ariel and Flounder returned to her secret cave so the little mermaid could be with her human treasures.

"Oh, Flounder," said Ariel. "Prince Eric's so handsome. I can hardly wait until I see him again."

Flounder just smiled. Ariel combed her hair with her dingelhopper and wished for the day when she would be with her human prince forever.

Mickey Mouse's Picnic

Mickey Mouse sang:

"What a beautiful day for a picnic,
What a picnical day for a lark!
In the happiest way
We frolic all day,
And we won't get back home until dark!"

Mickey was feeling very happy as he skipped up the walk to Minnie Mouse's house. "Ready, Minnie?" he called.

Pluto, Goofy, Daisy Duck, and Clarabelle Cow were waiting in Mickey's car.

"Ready!" Minnie said with a smile. Mickey peeked inside the lunch basket. Minnie had packed huge peanut butter and jelly sandwiches, cold meat sandwiches, deviled eggs, potato salad, radishes, onions, pink lemonade, and a great big chocolate cake!

"Let's go!" said Mickey. And he picked up the basket and led Minnie out to the car.

"It seems strange to go on a picnic without Donald Duck," said Mickey as they drove away.

"Yes, but there is always trouble when Donald is along," said the others.

When they were far down the road, none of them saw a figure come out from hiding and jump up and down in rage! It was Donald Duck!

"What a beautiful day for a picnic,
What a picnical day for a lark!"

everyone sang as Mickey Mouse drove merrily down the road to the picnic grounds.

And it did start out to be a perfect day. First they went for a walk along the riverbank. They

found a grassy spot beneath a tall shade tree. And they left Minnie's lunch basket there.

Then everyone went swimming in the old swimming hole. And how good that fresh, cool water felt! They swam, floated, played around, and had a wonderful time.

"I'm hungry enough to eat that whole basketful of lunch myself," Mickey said after a while.

"We'll see that you don't, Mickey!" Minnie laughed. "But it is time to eat, I guess."

So they all scrambled out of the water and hurried off to dress.

"Say!" Goofy cried. "Look at this, will you!" Goofy was holding up his pants. The legs were tied into knots. So were his shirtsleeves. And Mickey's were, too.

"Well, I never!" said Clarabelle Cow.

"Some mischief-maker must be around," Mickey said with a shake of his head.

But Minnie had a worse thought than that.

"The lunch!" she cried. And she ran up the bank to the shade of that big old tree.

The lunch basket was gone!

"Oh!" groaned everyone. "Not the lunch!"

"Hurry and get into your clothes, everybody!"

Mickey cried. "We'll soon find out about this."

They struggled to undo the knots in their clothes. Then they dressed in a flash and were off on the hunt.

All through the woods they hunted, under every bush and trailing vine. But not a sign of that lunch basket did they see.

At last they came out on the road again, near where they had left Mickey's car. They were hot and tired and hungry and cross.

And it was then that they met Donald Duck, walking along the road all by himself. He had a fishing pole over one shoulder. And a bundle hung from the end of the fishing pole.

Donald was whistling as he walked along, and he looked very pleased with himself.

"Well, hello, hello, hello!" he cried. "Imagine meeting you folks out here. I just came from some fishing myself. Got tired of spending a lonely day at home."

"Oh—er—yes," said Mickey. He felt bad because they had left Donald behind.

"Where are you folks going?" Donald asked.

"We are hunting for our lunch," Mickey said.

"For lunch?" said Donald. "Why, I have enough for us all in my bundle here. I will be glad to share it with my friends."

Now everyone felt guilty. But they were hungry, so they said thank you, they would like to eat with Donald.

Under the same big shady tree, Donald opened his bundle.

The lunch was delicious. There were peanut butter and jelly sandwiches, cold meat sandwiches, deviled eggs, potato salad, radishes, onions, pink lemonade, and a great big chocolate cake!

A strange look came into Mickey's and Minnie Mouse's eyes as they saw that picnic lunch. But they did not say a word.

So they all sat down and ate and ate.

"This is delicious, Donald," said Clarabelle Cow.

"And it is nice of you, too, Donald," Daisy Duck added, "to share it with us."

"Sure is," said Goofy, reaching for another sandwich.

"Yes," Mickey admitted. "I guess we misjudged you, Donald, old boy."

"Humph!" said Minnie Mouse. Then she turned to Donald with her sweetest smile.

"Did you bring a knife for cutting the chocolate cake, Donald?" she asked.

"Er—ah, I had one somewhere," Donald said. He looked all around, but he could not find it.

"I fastened a knife to the bottom of my cake pan with paper tape," Minnie said.

Mickey leaned over and looked at the bottom of the cake pan. And there, sure enough, was a knife, fastened to the bottom of the pan with paper tape. On the knife handle were the letters *M.M.*

"Well!" said Minnie.

"Why, Donald!" cried Daisy Duck.

"So that's where our lunch disappeared to!" cried Mickey Mouse.

Donald dropped his eyes. "I'm sorry, honest I am," he said. "I won't ever do it again."

"Where is my lunch basket?" Minnie asked.

"In Mickey's car," Donald admitted.

Mickey had to laugh. "Well," he said as he cut the cake, "we've all learned a lesson, I think. Donald won't snatch lunch baskets anymore. And we know it's better to bring Donald on a picnic."

Everyone had to laugh then. And they all piled back into Mickey's car. They made room for Donald to sit in the empty lunch basket.

Then away they went toward town, singing:

"In the happiest way
We will frolic all day,
And we won't get back
home until dark!"

Donald Duck and the Christmas Carol

"Deck the halls with boughs of holly!" sang Donald Duck and his nephews.

It was the day before Christmas. They had finished their Christmas shopping. They were busy trimming their Christmas tree when the doorbell rang.

"Merry Christmas! Merry Christmas!" cried Huey, Dewey, and Louie as they ran to open the door.

"Christmas is a waste of time and money," snapped Uncle Scrooge. "I came to see if you'd drive me out to my farm to bury these sacks of money I've saved up this year.

"You have no money saved up, I'll wager, after buying these fool presents. And it's clear to see you're set on wasting your time, too. So—Bah! Humbug! And good-bye to you!"

Out stamped Uncle Scrooge with his money

"Bah!" said Uncle Scrooge, shaking the snow from his coat as he stamped into the house. "Christmas? Humbug!"

"Christmas, humbug? Why, Uncle Scrooge! How can you say such a thing?" cried Huey, Dewey, and Louie Duck.

sacks. And off he went into the swirling snow.

"Wait, Uncle Scrooge!" called Donald.

"Merry Christmas, Uncle Scrooge," called Huey, Dewey, and Louie.

But Uncle Scrooge just grunted and shook his cane at the jolly crowds of Christmas shoppers.

Donald was right. Uncle Scrooge stamped home through the snow, all the way across town to his big old empty mansion.

He locked the door behind him. He drew all the curtains and shades.

Then he stamped up the stairs to his cold, dark room. And he propped himself up in bed with a book and a candle to read by.

"Christmas—humbug," he muttered to himself. "I don't care for anyone. And nobody cares for me. That's the way, if I had my say, that everyone would be!"

As the candle sputtered and shadows danced on the walls, Uncle Scrooge's head drooped over his book. He was almost asleep when a knock sounded at his door. In walked a figure dressed all in white, with a holly wreath on his head.

"Old skinflint!" cried Donald. "Trying to spoil our Christmas just because he won't have one of his own."

"Poor Uncle Scrooge! No Christmas at all! What will he do, Uncle Donald?" asked the boys.

"He'll go home and lock the door and draw the curtains and sit all alone in his dark, cold house, feeling sorry for himself," said Donald Duck.

"He will?" said the boys. "Say, why don't we—" and they turned back to their jolly Christmas tree.

In his hands he carried a big black book.

"Who—who are you?" asked Uncle Scrooge.

"I am the Spirit of Christmas Past," said the figure. "Do you remember the fun that you used to have at Christmastime?"

And, putting an old snapshot album into Scrooge's hand, the figure slipped out the door.

Uncle Scrooge turned the pages. "Why, here's Daisy!" he cried. "With the doll I gave her one year.

"And little Donald on his rocking horse! My, what fun we used to have! I wish—"

Uncle Scrooge was so busy with the snapshots that he did not hear the door open again. A second figure slipped into his room. This one was dressed in red.

"I am the Spirit of Christmas Present," said the figure. "Listen to the fun others have at Christmastime."

And outside the door Scrooge could hear happy voices singing,

"Deck the halls with boughs of holly,
Fa la la la la la la la la,
'Tis the season to be jolly,
Fa la la la la la la la la!"

"Bah—" Uncle Scrooge began. But he could not finish. Something caught in his throat. When he looked up again, a third figure was standing beside his bed.

"I am the Spirit of Christmas Yet to Come," said this figure, who was dressed in black. "If you do not mend your ways, you will never have a happy Christmas again."

"But what can I do?" cried Uncle Scrooge.

"Follow me!" said the figure. And Uncle Scrooge scrambled out of bed and followed him out of the gloomy room and down the long, dark stairs.

The figure turned toward the living room door.

"There's nothing in there but dust," said Uncle Scrooge. But he followed along anyway.

"Merry Christmas, Uncle Scrooge!" cried Daisy and Donald and the nephews, waiting in the living room.

There stood a beautiful Christmas tree. Around it was heaped the biggest pile of presents Uncle Scrooge had ever seen. And some of them were for him!

"When we finish opening presents," said Uncle Scrooge after a while, "let's take my sacks of money and give some to every person we see who doesn't look as if he's having as merry a Christmas as ours.

"For always remember this, boys! Christmas is the best day of all!"

Pinocchio

One night, long, long ago, the Evening Star shone down across the dark sky. Its beams formed a shimmering pathway to a tiny village whose humble little homes lay deep in sleep. Only one house still had a light burning in the window, and that was the workshop of Geppetto, the kindly old wood-carver. He was busily carving a puppet out of wood.

"At last he is finished!" cried Geppetto as he held the wooden boy high in the air.

"The only thing left to do now," said Geppetto to the puppet, "is to give you a name. Let's see . . . I shall call you Pinocchio!"

"What a grand name for such a handsome boy!" Jiminy Cricket said with a chirp.

But Geppetto's happiness soon faded, for deep in his heart he wished that Pinocchio were a real boy.

From his bed, Geppetto looked out into the night and saw the bright evening star. "Star light, star bright, first star I see tonight . . . I wish I may, I wish I might, have the wish I make tonight." With all his heart Geppetto wished that Pinocchio were a real boy. Then Geppetto drifted off to sleep.

Just then, a flash of light burst across the sky as

a fairy flew straight from the evening star into Geppetto's house.

"Good Geppetto," whispered the Blue Fairy, "you have given so much happiness to others, you deserve to have your wish come true." Then, with a wave of her wand, the Blue Fairy brought Pinocchio to life.

Jiminy Cricket watched in amazement as Pinocchio began to walk and talk.

"A-a-am I a REAL boy?" Pinocchio asked the Blue Fairy.

"No, Pinocchio," she answered. "First you must prove yourself to be brave, truthful, and unselfish. You must also learn to choose between right and wrong."

"But how will I know what is right or wrong?" he asked.

"Your conscience will tell you," said the Blue Fairy.

"What's a conscience?" asked Pinocchio.

"That's the small voice that people don't always listen to," Jiminy Cricket answered with a chirp.

"Yes," said the Blue Fairy. She made Jiminy Cricket kneel down before her, and she dubbed him Pinocchio's Official Conscience. It was his job to see that Pinocchio did only what was right. Then the Blue Fairy vanished.

When Geppetto awoke, he could not believe his eyes.

"My wish has come true!" he shouted. "Pinocchio is alive!" Although Geppetto soon realized that Pinocchio was still made out of wood, it mattered little to him.

"I shall love you just the way you are," he told Pinocchio. Then he explained that Pinocchio must go to school, like all boys. And so, that very morning, Pinocchio happily set off.

Pinocchio hadn't gone very far when Gideon, a cat, and Foulfellow, a sly fox, saw him. Foulfellow thought, "A wooden boy with no strings. I'll bet Stromboli, the puppeteer, would pay a pretty price for him." Foulfellow convinced Pinocchio that acting was the life for him—and sold him to Stromboli.

That night, after Pinocchio had performed to rounds of applause, Stromboli locked him away in a cage.

"How am I ever going to get out of this horrible place?" sobbed Pinocchio.

Just then a voice called out, "Don't worry, Pinoke, I'll save you!" It was Jiminy Cricket! He pulled, pushed, and shook the lock, but he couldn't get Pinocchio out.

Suddenly the Blue Fairy appeared once more.

"Pinocchio, why didn't you go to school?" she asked.

"I…uh…was brought here by a big green monster who was going to cook me for his supper," he lied. Pinocchio's nose began to grow and grow.

"You're lying, Pinocchio," said the Blue Fairy sadly, "and it's as plain as the nose on your face."

"Please give him one more chance," pleaded Jiminy Cricket. "I'll make sure he never lies again."

"One more chance, that's all you'll have," said the Blue Fairy, and she set Pinocchio free. He

promised never to lie again, and he headed straight for school.

But on the way Pinocchio was stopped by Foulfellow once more.

"And where are you going on such a fine day?" he said with a sneer.

"To school," replied Pinocchio.

"Ha! School is no place for a boy like you!" said Foulfellow, laughing. "If you follow me, I'll show you a place that's much more fun—Pleasure Island!"

"Don't go, Pinoke!" warned Jiminy Cricket. But Pinocchio did not listen, and before he knew it Foulfellow had sold him to the mean old driver of the Pleasure Island stagecoach.

The coach was pulled by six unhappy donkeys. The coachman went from village to village, buying up all the boys he could. Once the coach was full, he headed to the ferry bound for Pleasure Island.

Pinocchio sat beside a loudmouthed boy named Lampwick. "Don't worry about a thing," Lampwick said with a chuckle. "Once we get to Pleasure Island, we won't have to listen to anyone or worry about what's right or wrong!"

On Pleasure Island Pinocchio forgot everything the Blue Fairy had told him. He fought with the other boys, smoked corncob pipes, tossed rocks through windows, and yelled and screamed with all his might. Then he followed Lampwick down Tobacco Lane to the Pool Hall.

"This is a great place, Lampwick!" shouted Pinocchio.

But as Pinocchio turned to his friend, he could not believe his eyes. Lampwick had suddenly grown long ears and a tail. Lampwick had turned into a donkey!

Pinocchio felt the top of his head and looked down at his behind. He, too, had sprouted donkey's ears and a tail! Now he knew where the coachman got his tired, sad-looking donkeys.

"Come with me before it's too late!" cried Jiminy Cricket, who had quietly followed Pinocchio to Pleasure Island.

As fast as they could, Pinocchio and Jiminy Cricket ran through the gates of Pleasure Island and jumped off the cliffs into the sea.

Pinocchio and Jiminy Cricket swam all the way back to land and rushed to Geppetto's house.

But when they arrived, Geppetto was gone.

"Maybe something awful happened to him!" cried Pinocchio.

Just then, a beautiful white dove dropped a note from high in the sky.

"It's from Geppetto," said Jiminy Cricket, "and it says that he went looking for you and was swallowed by a whale named Monstro. He's alive, but he's trapped inside the whale."

"I must find him!" cried Pinocchio. Pinocchio and Jiminy Cricket leapt into the sea to start their search. Soon they spotted Monstro and got as close as they could to the snoring whale.

So they built a fire, and the smoke tickled Monstro's nose till he let out a huge sneeze. Pinocchio and Geppetto were sent flying out to sea on their tiny raft.

But then Monstro came charging after the raft. Soon Monstro caught up with the raft and splintered it with one blow of his powerful tail.

Geppetto was sinking. "Never mind about me!" he cried. "Save yourself, my son!"

Suddenly Monstro opened his eyes and mouth and gulped down a school of fish. Pinocchio was swallowed along with them. Inside the whale, Geppetto was fishing. He felt a tug on his line and reeled it in. Pinocchio was at the other end!

"My son! My son!" shouted Geppetto. "I thought I'd never see you again!"

"I missed you so, Father," said Pinocchio. "I've been a bad boy and I'm sorry."

"That's all right, my son," said Geppetto. "The important thing is for all of us to get out of here safely."

"I have an idea!" cried Pinocchio. "Let's build a fire! It'll make Monstro sneeze us right out of here."

But Pinocchio swam back to Geppetto and helped him stay afloat. Geppetto was washed safely ashore, but Pinocchio did not fare as well. Geppetto found him lying in the water among the rocks, lifeless.

Geppetto took Pinocchio home. As he wept a soft voice said, "Pinocchio, you've proved yourself brave, truthful, and unselfish. Now you will be a real boy."

Pinocchio moved and blinked his eyes. He was alive—and no longer wooden. Geppetto danced for joy.

Jiminy Cricket was happy, too. In Pinocchio he had sure proof that when you wish upon a star, your dreams come true!

The Aristocats

In Madame Bonfamille's fine home in Paris, all was peaceful. Well, almost...

"Me first!" Kitten Marie shouted. "I'm a lady!"

"Ha! You're not a lady," said her brother Toulouse.

"You're just a sister," said Berlioz.

"I'll show you!" Marie shouted.

Marie started after her brothers. A chase began that brought giggles and then tears as Marie's tail somehow arrived in Berlioz's mouth.

"Children!" said Duchess, their mother.

"I was just practicing my biting, Mamma," said Berlioz.

"Aristocats do not bite," said Duchess. "Come, let's practice being ladies and gentlemen."

Soon all was peaceful again—but not for long. Out in the kitchen, someone was planning to do something bad to the Aristocats.

Edgar the butler had heard Madame say, "I'm leaving my fortune to my dear cats. Edgar may have what's left when they're gone."

Edgar had thought, "Four cats. Nine lives each. Four times nine is...is...too long. They'll outlive me, unless..."

And, right then and there, Edgar planned a way to make the Aristocats disappear.

"Come, kitties," he called. "Come taste this delicious *crème de la Edgar*."

It *was* delicious. Their friend Roquefort the mouse thought so, too. But...everyone who drank it fell asleep!

And the Aristocats slept so soundly that they didn't know they left home in a basket on Edgar's motorcycle. They didn't know that Edgar was chased by dogs, and that the basket fell off and landed under a bridge.

They didn't know they were alone, far out in the country, until a storm broke and they woke up.

"Mamma!" Marie called out. "I'm afraid! Where are we?"

"I don't know, darling. I...I...Let's just try to sleep until morning."

But Duchess couldn't sleep. All she could do was worry.

Then she heard a rough voice singing, "I'm O'Malley the Alley Cat. Helpin' ladies is my—"

"Oh, Mr. O'Malley, can you help me?" Duchess called. "I'm in great trouble. I'm lost."

O'Malley bowed. "Yer ladyship, I'll fly you off on my magic carpet for two."

Berlioz popped up. So did Toulouse. And Marie. "What magic carpet?" they asked.

"Uh...er..." O'Malley stammered. Then he grinned. "Look, I said magic carpet for two, but it can be a magic carpet for *five* also." He made an X on the road. "It'll stop for passengers right here. Watch!"

They watched. Soon something came down the road. O'Malley made himself big and scary-looking and jumped out in front of it. The something stopped right on the X.

"All aboard!" said O'Malley. "One magic carpet, ready to go."

"Aw, it's just a truck," said Berlioz.

"Shh!" said Duchess. Then she smiled at O'Malley. "It's a lovely magic carpet. Is it going to Paris?" she asked.

"It's going somewhere," said O'Malley, helping her on.

But soon the driver of the magic carpet saw that he had passengers. He stopped with a jerk. He shouted terrible things, and when he threw a heavy wrench at his passengers, they jumped to safety.

"What an awful man!" said Duchess. "I wish we were home."

"Humans are like that," said O'Malley.

"Oh, no, Mr. O'Malley," said Duchess. "*My* humans aren't like that."

"Hmm!" said O'Malley. "Then how did you get here? Somebody doesn't like you."

Duchess thought about that as they began the long walk back to Paris.

Finally they arrived in the city, so tired they could hardly take a step.

"We'll stop and rest at my peaceful pad," O'Malley said.

But the peaceful pad was bouncing with sound. "Oh...uh...some friends have stopped by," O'Malley explained. "We'll go somewhere—"

"I'd like to meet your friends, Mr. O'Malley," said Duchess.

So O'Malley introduced all his swinging musician friends. What fun it was! They played for the four Aristocats, and Duchess sang for them.

Then, after the children were tucked in, Duchess and O'Malley talked.

"Your friends are delightful," said Duchess.

"How about sharin' them with me?" asked Mr. O'Malley. "I mean, how about stayin' here with me? Like forever."

Marie heard him. She whispered, "Oh, Mr. O'Malley's going to be our father...maybe."

"Great!" said Toulouse.

"Shh!" said Marie. "Listen!"

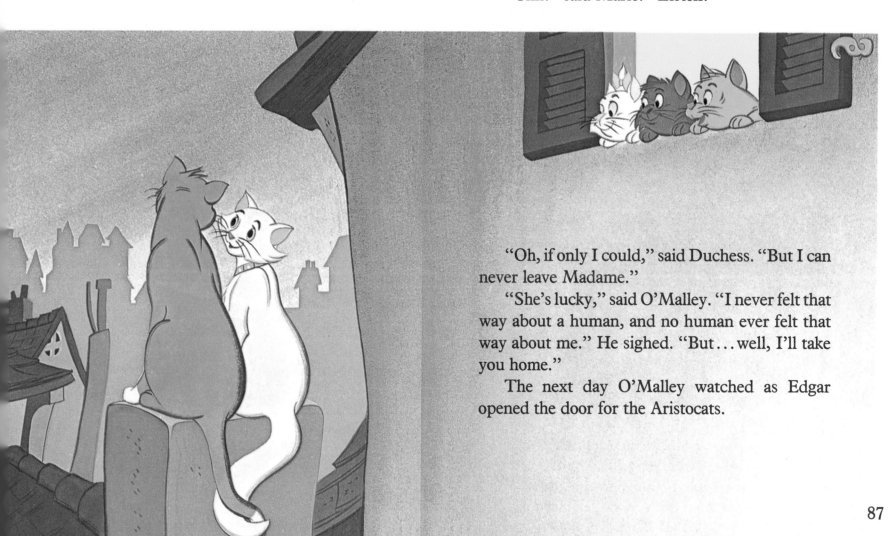

"Oh, if only I could," said Duchess. "But I can never leave Madame."

"She's lucky," said O'Malley. "I never felt that way about a human, and no human ever felt that way about me." He sighed. "But...well, I'll take you home."

The next day O'Malley watched as Edgar opened the door for the Aristocats.

"Now," Edgar said, "you're going in this trunk to Timbuktu and *never* coming back! Onto the baggage truck you go and away forever." He opened the door.

But suddenly alley cats were everywhere. Two unlocked the trunk and let out the Aristocats.

And some, with a little help, put Edgar inside. Now someone else was on his way to Timbuktu!

And there were some happy cats who were very glad to stay home. Listen! You can hear a rough voice, and a lovely soft voice, and three little voices singing...

"We're Mr. and Mrs. O'Malley. We're the *five* Aristocats."

"Oh!" said Edgar. "You're back! I mean... uh, how *nice* to see you back!"

"Looks like they don't need me anymore," said O'Malley. He turned away sadly.

But O'Malley was wrong. The first thing Edgar did was put Duchess and her children into a bag. Then, when he heard Madame call, "Are my little dears back? Did I hear them come in?" Edgar popped the bag of cats into the nearest container and went to answer Madame's call.

The four Aristocats were stiff with fear. What would happen to them now? Then Duchess remembered Roquefort the mouse. "Get O'Malley!" she called. She told him how to find her friend. "Hurry!"

Roquefort ran out, just as Edgar came back in with a trunk.

88

The Jungle Book

Based on the Mowgli stories by Rudyard Kipling

Many strange legends are told of the jungles of far-off India. They speak of Bagheera the black panther, of Baloo the bear. They tell of Kaa the sly python, and of the lord of the jungle, the great tiger Shere Khan. But of all the legends none is so strange as the story of a small boy named Mowgli.

The story began when a child, left all alone in the jungle, was found by Bagheera the panther. He could not give the small, helpless "man-cub" care and nourishment, so Bagheera took him to the den of a wolf family with young cubs of their own.

That is how it happened that Mowgli, as the man-cub came to be called, was raised among the wolves. All the jungle folk were his friends.

Bagheera took Mowgli on long walks and taught him jungle lore.

Baloo the bumbling bear played games with Mowgli and taught him to live a life of ease. There were coconuts for the cracking, bananas for the peeling, sweet and juicy pawpaws to pick from jungle trees.

Hathi, the proud old leader of the elephant herd, tried to train young Mowgli in military drill as he led his troop trumpeting down the jungle trails.

Sly old Kaa the python would have loved to have squeezed Mowgli tight in his coils. But Mowgli's friends warned him against Kaa.

It was Shere Khan the tiger who was the real danger to Mowgli. That was because Shere Khan, like all tigers, had a hatred of man.

Ten times the season of rains had come to the jungle where Mowgli made his home with the wolf family. Then Shere Khan returned to the wolves' hunting grounds.

The wolf pack met at Council Rock when next the moon was full.

So it was arranged, and when the greenish light of the jungle morning slipped through the leaves, Bagheera and Mowgli set out.

All day they walked, and when night fell, they slept on a high branch of a giant banyan tree. All this seemed like an adventure to Mowgli. But when he learned that he was to leave the jungle, he was horrified.

"No!" cried Mowgli. "The jungle is my home. I can take care of myself. I will stay!"

He slipped down a length of trailing vine and rudely ran away.

For a while Mowgli marched with Hathi and the elephants. But he soon tired of that.

Then he found Baloo bathing in a jungle pool. Mowgli joined him for a dip.

Suddenly down swooped the monkey folk, the noisy, foolish *Bandar-log*. They had snatched Mowgli from the pool before Baloo knew what was happening.

"As you know," said Akela, the leader of the pack, "Shere Khan the tiger has returned. If he learns that our pack is harboring a man-cub, danger will be doubled for all our families. Are we agreed that the man-cub must go?"

Out from the shadows stepped Bagheera the panther.

"I brought the man-cub to the pack," he said. "It is my duty to see him safely out of the jungle. I know a man-village not far away where he will be well cared for."

They tossed him through the air from hand to hand and swung him away through the trees.

Off in the jungle, Bagheera heard Mowgli's cry and came with a leap and a bound.

"The monkeys have stolen Mowgli away!" gasped Baloo.

Off raced Bagheera and Baloo to the ruined city where the monkeys made their home.

They found Mowgli a prisoner of the monkey king.

"Teach me the secret of fire," the monkey king ordered Mowgli. "The magic of fire will frighten even Shere Kahn. With it I shall be the equal of men. Until I know the secret, you are my prisoner."

It took quite a fight for Bagheera and Baloo to rescue Mowgli that time!

"Now you see," they told him, "why you must go to the man-village to be safe."

But alas, that foolish boy would not understand. He kicked up his heels and ran away again.

This time his wanderings led him to where Shere Khan lay waiting in the high grass, smiling a hungry smile.

When Mowgli caught sight of the tiger, Shere Khan asked, "Well, man-cub, aren't you going to run?"

But Mowgli did not have the wisdom to be afraid. "Why should I run?" he asked, staring Shere Khan in the eye as the tiger gathered himself for a spring. "I'm not afraid of you."

"That foolish boy!" growled Bagheera, who had crept close just in time to hear Mowgli.

Both Bagheera and Baloo flung themselves upon the lord of the jungle, to save Mowgli once more. They were brave and strong, but the tiger was mighty of tooth and claw.

There was a flash of lightning and a dead tree nearby caught fire. Mowgli snatched a burning branch and waved it in Shere Khan's face. The tiger, terrified, ran away. Mowgli was very pleased with himself as he strutted between the two weary warriors, Bagheera and Baloo.

Suddenly Mowgli stopped. From ahead came a sound that was strange to him. He peeked through the brush. It was the song of a village girl who had come to fill her water jar.

As he listened to the soft notes of her song, Mowgli felt strange inside. He felt that he must follow her. Mowgli crept up the path to the village, following the girl and her song.

Baloo and Bagheera watched the small figure as long as it could be seen. When Mowgli vanished inside the village gate, Bagheera sighed a deep sigh.

"It is just as it should be, Baloo," he said. "Our Mowgli is safe in the man-village at last. He's with his own people now. He has found his true home."